The Christmas Cabin

Flight to Freedom Series

The Glass Bottom Boat-1
The Lighthouse Baby-2
The Orphan Beach-3
The Christmas Cabin-4
Snow Globe Secrets-5

The Christmas Cabin

By

Laura Thomas

Dedication:

For my dear mum, Gwendoline Anne…

Lover of Christmas and cabins.

"The Lord himself goes before you and will be with you;
he will never leave you nor forsake you.
Do not be afraid; do not be discouraged."

Deuteronomy 31:8 (NIV)

Acknowledgments

What an absolute joy to write my first Christmas novella—and to bring the story to my home province in Canada! My heartfelt thanks to:

Mountain Brook Ink—my publisher who believes in me enough to publish my fourth book in the series. Thanks for allowing me to continue the "Flight to Freedom" storyline…

Candee Fick—my editor extraordinaire who makes everything sparkle and shine. You are my very own Christmas fairy!

Blossom Turner—my wonderful, whip-smart critique partner and friend.

Rhys Williams—my Welsh nephew who truly adores Christmas. I had to use your name!

Charlotte, Jameson, and Jacob—for all our fun, fabulous family Christmases.

Lyndon—my husband, who began a Canadian adventure with me so many years ago, snowshoes with me, and assures me no bears are following, and gives me all the romantic inspiration I need for writing these books! I love you!

My Heavenly Father—for giving me light and life and words.

Chapter One

"Home sweet home."

Carla swallowed her whispered words. Would Hollybrook *ever* feel sweet again?

Standing on the snow-covered curb, fists clenched, she fought the urge to retreat back inside the airport and hop on the next plane out of the frozen city she once adored. A chill deeper than the current frigid temperature settled in her chest. *Coming home for Christmas… what was I thinking?*

A rolling suitcase rammed into her thigh. She winced and looked up into the angular face of a twenty-something guy bundled in trendy snow gear. Her nostrils tingled with an excess of musky aftershave.

He flashed a confident smile and raised a brow.

Panic flowed through her veins as she nudged her own case between the two of them. "Sorry." She sidestepped a patch of ice, and her teeth chattered an automatic apology before she could question why *she* was the one apologizing.

"No problem, sweetheart." He winked and ambled off toward a line of waiting taxis.

Carla released the breath she'd been holding. *Calm down, girl.* She would be a nervous wreck by the end of the day if she suspected every guy in town. Life was so much simpler back at the orphanage in Mexico…

Secluded. Sheltered. Safe.

She tucked wayward strands of long hair behind her ears and plunged trembling hands into the pockets of her leather jacket. A stomp of her boots helped her feel her toes again. *I can do this. I can do this. I can do this.*

Ping.

A text message. She pulled her phone from the carry-on bag slung over her shoulder. A message from him. Her heart raced.

HEY, CARLA. I'M HERE IN HOLLYBROOK. WONDERING IF YOUR FLIGHT MADE IT IN OKAY. JUST CHECKING YOU STILL WANT TO DO THIS TONIGHT?

Her mouth was bone dry. She tucked the phone in her pocket, slid a water bottle from her bag, and chugged the cool liquid. Weird how flying always made her feel like she'd traveled the Sahara. Dry skin, dry mouth. Yes, she still wanted to meet tonight. She had to see him before she lost her courage. Besides, this conversation was the only way for her to move forward. To heal from the hurt—and the truth he knew nothing about. She stuffed the water bottle back into her bag and retrieved the phone.

HI, RHYS. YES, FLIGHTS WERE BOTH ON TIME. MIRACLE OF MIRACLES. WAITING FOR MY SISTER AT THE AIRPORT. FORGOT HOW COLD BRITISH COLUMBIA WAS IN DECEMBER! LET'S MEET TONIGHT AS PLANNED. WHAT TIME CAN YOU GET TO THE CABIN?

Did that sound too needy? Too desperate? Oh well, too late now…

SEVEN O'CLOCK?

As long as she could persuade her sister she would be safe at the cabin.

She nibbled on her lower lip. Alexis had been shocked when Carla messaged to say she was coming for Christmas. Alexis would totally pull the bossy-big-sis card when she discovered Carla wanted to stay at the cabin alone tonight. Face her demons. Where *was* Alexis anyway? Carla glanced at her phone to check the time. Most likely running late. Busy with clients. Or perhaps Alexis had forgotten about picking her up—the big sister's reaction to the prodigal daughter's return? Although, that would require her parents to actually be here…

"Carla?"

Alexis? Carla spun around at the sound of the familiar voice and was enveloped in a bear hug and the nostalgic scent of jasmine. As they swayed back and forth for several beats, Carla basked in the bond they shared despite their differences, and her shoulders relaxed. She pulled back and peered up several inches. Immaculate, as always. Her sister's wavy blonde hair had grown longer since they were last together—almost as long as Carla's now. Alexis's make-up was flawless, and her fitted navy coat screamed professional and expensive. The most put-together young woman in Hollybrook.

"You look great, Lex." Carla buried her phone in her pocket.

"Thanks." Alexis's eyes skimmed over Carla's head. "Your hair seems lighter. Did you color it?"

Carla cringed at just how messy her bun must be after two flights. "No, it gets less mousey when I'm in the sun all day long. That's all."

"Right. Nice. Have you been waiting long? I had a house showing. Are you hungry?" Another tight hug. "I can't believe my baby sister's home for Christmas. It's going to be amazing. Even if it's only for a few days."

"I know. It's a fleeting visit, but thanks for picking me up."

Alexis grabbed the suitcase and led the way. "Of course. Let's get going. The truck's close by." She tugged the stylish wool coat tighter over her pantsuit. "It's freezing out here."

"Tell me about it." Carla tucked her chin beneath a soft wool scarf, grateful she'd thought to pop it inside her hand baggage. "I've gone from T-shirts to toques in a matter of hours." Her heart squeezed as she recalled the tearful farewells from the darlings she cared for back at the orphanage.

"You want me to stop for coffee or anything? Warm you up?"

"I'm good, but thanks." *I want to get to the cabin.*

Alexis unlocked her truck and stowed the luggage in the backseat on the passenger side. "It's about time you experienced a Canadian white Christmas again. I feel like you've missed at least five."

"Four."

"Whatever." Alexis flicked her hair behind her shoulders and strode around to the driver's side.

Carla opened the passenger door and climbed in. "It's four. I was here five Christmases ago." She slammed the door and met her sister's gaze across the wide console. "You're always welcome to stay with me in Sonaja and have Christmas on the beach. You might enjoy it. Sea, sand, screaming kids…"

"Exactly." Alexis looked like she'd sucked on a lemon.

Carla tugged the seat belt into place. "You know the thought of Christmas here is…"

"Difficult. I get it, but you have to move on. I only want what's best for you. You know that, right?" Alexis reached over and squeezed Carla's hand and then grimaced. "Your fingers are like icicles. I hope you brought some practical clothes for our winter. If not, you'll have to make do with something of mine."

The truck rumbled to life, and a stream of warm air gushed into Carla's face. "That would be interesting. You're what—five inches taller than me? But thanks. Actually, I was hoping my stuff might still be stashed at the cabin." She rubbed her hands together. "Including gloves."

"I haven't thrown any of your things out, so you should be set. Unless you want to change your mind and stay with me at my house."

Carla defogged her glasses with the scarf. "I get that you aren't keen on me staying at the cabin, but I want to. I need to."

"Are you sure? I mean, it's your call." Alexis pulled out onto the road that would take them through town.

"Yes. No. I don't know. It just seems like the only way I can move forward with a future is to work through the past." How cliché did that sound? She closed her eyes for a moment and breathed in the pungent leather scent of a brand-new vehicle interior. Alexis was doing well as a realtor. No surprise there.

"Okay, but you're still welcome to come and crash with me and Lily. We've got oodles of room."

"I know." Carla chuckled. "That English bulldog is totally your child."

"Of course, she is. You do *actual* children—lots of them, in fact, and I do dogs. Well, one dog. Seriously, can you even imagine me with a real-life child to take care of? Although some days it feels like Lily is needier than a human baby."

"I'm sure." Carla stared through the windshield and pictured the children's smiling faces back at the orphanage. What would they make of this snow? They'd never experienced a real winter. She relaxed into the seat as they passed a row of boutique hotels, all decked with colored lights and oversized wreaths. Even the fire station looked festive with its swags of greenery gracing the bay doors and a gigantic inflatable snowman in the parking lot. Several pedestrians navigated the icy sidewalks, and one lost her footing and slid through a pile of snow right into the—

"Watch out!" Carla screeched the words and flung an arm across the central console toward her sister.

Alexis hit the brakes and gained traction on the layer of salt over the snow-covered street. "What on earth?"

A skinny young woman scurried the rest of the way across the road, huge headphones covering her ears, oblivious to the fact that she was almost mowed down.

"For heaven's sake." Alexis honked the horn, but the girl didn't flinch. "That's Sarah-Jane Knight. You remember her from high school? Her brother was in my class, but she was… maybe a couple of years younger than you." She thrust the truck back into drive and continued on.

Carla swiveled around and watched the girl shuffle along the snowy sidewalk, head down. "Yeah, I think so. Super shy. Tons of siblings."

"Right. She's Sarah-Jane Tremblay now. Married to Richard. They have a little place on the lake."

"Didn't his family own a property there when we were kids?"

"Yeah. I think he inherited it when old Mr. Tremblay passed. Something like that." Alexis lifted a shoulder.

"Does David what's-his-name still live here? The one who was in love with you since kindergarten?"

Alexis snorted. "David Baxter. Yes, he's a cop here in town, and he's still besotted with me. Plus, that super smart guy who followed you around like a puppy in high school…"

"Oh, you mean Gary Smithers? Please tell me he found someone. He was sweet, even if I had zero interest in him."

"Married your old friend Kim, and they have, wait for it"—a cackle escaped her lips—"triplets."

"Yikes. I adore kids, but three all at once…"

Alexis shook her head. "Nightmarish."

"I almost forgot what it's like to live in a small town where everyone knows everyone."

The charm of twinkling Christmas lights draped on trees lining the road on Main Street brought back a cornucopia of memories. Some good, some horrific.

"Last chance to come and stay with me." Alexis pointed at the next set of traffic lights. "I'm up there on the right in the swanky neighborhood."

Carla recognized the intersection. A few new office buildings had appeared in the past five years, but she found a measure of comfort in the otherwise familiar surroundings. She glanced to where a new subdivision sprawled up the side of one of the smaller mountains. "Wow. You must have a stellar view."

"The best."

Carla grinned. Her sister was always the one who wanted the fancy things in life. With ex-missionary parents who became teachers with a long-term plan of returning to India once their own kids were independent, Alexis wanted none of that. She'd been determined to make something of herself, have a successful career, beautiful home, travel—the complete opposite of Carla.

"You could stay with me one night. When is this Madison arriving?" A slight edge clipped the name *Madison.*

"She's flying in tomorrow. I'd like to get settled at the cabin first." *And I have someone you do not approve of coming to see me this evening.*

"Fine. The cabin it is then."

Carla squinted as the winter sunshine broke through a layer of clouds and reflected off the snowbanks on either side of the road.

"Pass my shades? They're in the dash." Alexis held out her hand.

Carla dug the sunglasses out, wishing hers weren't in the bowels of her suitcase.

"I'm looking forward to meeting Madison, at last. I can't believe that yummy boss of yours got married."

"Yeah, Luke and Madison are the perfect couple. Besides, Madison and I have become like—"

"Sisters?" Alexis raised a shapely eyebrow.

Carla adjusted her glasses. "Yeah, something like that." Maybe Madison's visit hadn't been the best idea, after all. Yet, Madison had been so keen to visit Hollybrook for a few days before the three of them—Madison, Luke, and Carla—flew to Seattle for their big Christmas fundraising party.

"Is it her first time in Canada?"

Carla shook her head. "She's been elsewhere in B.C. Maybe Vancouver? She's never experienced a white Christmas before."

"That we can do in spades." Alexis twiddled the volume knob, and soft Christmas carols filled the cab. They passed more familiar landmarks—the bakery, bank, movie theatre—all covered in snow as if they'd been topped with generous dollops of whipped cream. A warmth filled Carla's chest. *Perhaps this won't be so awful.*

And there was her beloved library. The place where she first ran into Rhys Templeton as an idealistic twenty-two-year-old girl fresh from graduating university. She blinked back tears. The place she realized love at first sight was a thing.

They drove through another set of traffic lights and took the next left leading them out of town and up toward the cabin.

"If you need to grab a catnap, it's going to be a good half an hour before we're at the lake. I'm guessing you're exhausted after your flights."

Carla leaned back on the headrest. "Maybe I will. I have a feeling these next few days are going to be emotionally draining."

A few strains of "Silent Night" floated in the air.

Alexis cleared her throat. "I know you've come back to deal with some stuff that happened. That's all healthy and good. But I don't want to overstep or say the wrong thing with Madison. How much does she know exactly?"

Carla bit the inside of her cheek until she tasted the metallic tang of blood. "She knows my boyfriend dumped me on Christmas Eve five years ago at the cabin."

"And the rest?" Alexis's voice was a tender whisper. "The other thing that happened at the cabin?"

"I haven't told her yet. You're the only one who knows the rest. Unless you count my counsellor." Carla shut her eyes tight and exhaled. "Just you, me, and God."

Chapter Two

"HEY, SLEEPYHEAD. WE'RE HERE."

Carla blinked open gritty eyes, amazed she had fallen asleep. That's what a week's worth of restless nights did for a person.

"You must have been exhausted. They work you too hard at the orphanage." Alexis unlatched the driver's door and hopped out. She opened up the back and leaned across to grab the case from the passenger side of the seat. "I don't know how you can be around so many kids twenty-four-seven. Makes me tired thinking about it."

Carla rolled her shoulders and braced herself for the cold air. "You know I love it more than anything. It brings me to life." She grabbed her bag and jumped out, her suede ankle boots sinking into the snow. *Please let my snow boots still be in the closet.* "I can manage the case, Lex."

"I've got it."

Of course, you have. Carla lifted her gaze to familiar surroundings and expelled a contented sigh. The view was as picturesque as she remembered. To the right, their warm chestnut-colored cabin nestled beneath snow-laden pine trees dressed white like the tallest brides. Beyond them, mountains sloped up to the heavens as a majestic backdrop. She stepped in front of the truck, and to the left, the frozen lake spread before her on the other side of the driveway, dotted with more cabin homes than she remembered from five years ago.

This lake was the outlook she enjoyed from their large front porch every season of her growing up years.

"Still looks the same, hey?" A muffled scrape caused Carla to refocus as Alexis dragged the case over the snow-packed driveway toward the porch. "I wanted to keep the outside as authentic as possible. Rustic, cozy, a diamond in the rough, but wait until you see inside."

"Wait, what? You didn't tell me you redecorated." A bubble of panic rose from Carla's stomach. She'd envisioned how this would go, play-by-play. She knew this cabin, every square inch. Put her own blood, sweat, and so many tears into making the space livable when she came back from university. "After the months I spent fixing it up before I left for Mexico?"

"That was five years ago, and you didn't exactly finish the job. Don't worry, sis. You're going to love it. I had everything professionally renovated last spring. I wanted it to be ready for renting season over the summer, and it paid off because I was able to charge way more. Don't scowl; I wanted to surprise you."

Carla wasn't listening anymore. She concentrated on not slipping as she took faltering steps toward the front porch. Someone had swept the path clear of snow, and a glorious wreath of holly graced the bright blue door. At least that hadn't changed. The door had always been blue, ever since she could remember. She reached out and placed the palm of her hand on the smooth wood. *I'm back.*

"Here, let me unlock it." Alexis elbowed her out of the way and pushed the door ajar. "Give me a sec? I'll switch on the fire and lights so you can appreciate the full effect." She was enjoying this way too much.

"Go ahead then, Miss Realtor. Leave the case with me." The perfect opportunity to reply to Rhys. Carla heard the door close, pulled her phone from her coat pocket, and began typing.

HEY, RHYS. I'M ACTUALLY AT THE CABIN! AFTER ALL THESE YEARS, IT'S STILL THE SAME FROM THE OUTSIDE. I'M CURRENTLY LOOKING OUT AT THE LAKE AND IT FEELS LIKE MAYBE THIS PLACE HAS FROZEN IN TIME. APPARENTLY, ALEXIS HAS GIVEN THE INTERIOR A MAKEOVER—I GUESS YOU'LL BE ABLE TO SEE IT SOON ENOUGH. 7PM IS PERFECT. SEE YOU LATER.

She shivered and stomped her feet as she paced on the wooden boards. A ping sounded from her phone.

I SEEM TO RECALL A NOT-SO-GRACEFUL ICE-SKATING PERFORMANCE I ATTEMPTED TO IMPRESS YOU WITH ON THAT LAKE ONCE UPON A TIME. THINK I'LL GIVE IT A MISS THIS YEAR. LOOKING FORWARD TO SEEING THE CABIN AGAIN. OF COURSE, TO SEEING YOU.

Carla gulped down any hint of emotion and stuffed the phone back in her pocket. She would need to be strong when she saw him tonight. Before that even happened, she'd somehow have to explain to Alexis that she was meeting with Rhys. Alexis would not approve. No way.

She shook her head. For goodness's sake, Carla was a twenty-seven-year-old woman. Her parents were on the other side of the globe, and she certainly didn't need the approval of her big sister. She stared back at the lake. *I do need some guidance from God.*

Was she doing the right thing, agreeing to meet up with the only man she had ever loved? The one who left her on a Christmas Eve that would be forever etched in the darkest parts of her soul?

The lake. Focus on the lake. She puffed a long breath into the chilly air and observed the familiar vista as she leaned against the rough log wall, drawing strength from her fondest childhood memories.

In the summer, the lake would glisten a stunning turquoise. She'd spend entire days swimming, playing, and floating—when she didn't have her head buried in a book. As teachers, her parents always had summers off, and so the family would vacate their little house close to town and come here for a good chunk of time. Then they'd return here again for the crisp Thanksgiving long weekend—she could almost smell her mom's pumpkin pie wafting from inside. Her favorite time at the cabin was Christmas. This sweet log home was… magical. Her grandpa built it back in the day, and then her grandparents lived here full-time for some years. There was so much history sewn into the fabric of this place, so much she loved about it until—

"Ready."

Carla blinked and pivoted to see her sister's beaming face.

"Go ahead. Take a look." Alexis shifted the case out of the way and stood aside. "I dare you to tell me you don't love it."

Carla pushed the door wide open, and it swung in like an arm beckoning her to step inside.

A garland of fresh greenery threaded with white twinkly lights drew her eye up the renovated staircase before her. "Pretty."

"Wait until you see the bathroom up there. You're in for a treat."

"Still the two bedrooms?"

"Yeah. We didn't change the footprint of the place. Just made everything fantastic."

Carla grinned. The entry didn't seem much different as she dumped her bag on the tile floor and slid off snowy boots, leaving them on the rubber tray. Alexis closed the door behind her and situated the case at the bottom of the stairs.

Two steps into the great room, Carla stopped. The dark log walls had been painted a fresh white, and the place appeared twice its original size. "Oh my." The transformation was spectacular.

"Told you."

Light flooded the space through new, larger windows. "It's gorgeous. Absolutely gorgeous." Carla clutched her hands over her heart and turned in a circle, absorbing every delightful detail.

Soft fur throws and cream knitted blankets adorned two gray leather love seats. Carla swallowed down a lump of emotion as she wondered what had become of Grandma's handmade quilts. Carla made a mental note to dig through closets later. Instead, she focused on the real tiny Christmas trees that sat in baskets scattered in perfect placement around the room. "I don't know how you did it, but somehow it's both brighter and cozier at the same time."

"Right?" Alexis walked over to the fireplace. "This looks like the real deal, but it's all the warmth needed"—she pointed to a knob on the wall—"at the flick of a switch."

"Wow. Nice touch with a basket of real logs." Bringing in the firewood from the pile outside had never been her favorite chore. "I adore the stockings." Three chunky, knitted, cream stockings hung on the mantel along with white twinkly lights and more fresh greenery. "Oh, but you kept Grandpa's mantel?" She smiled as she smoothed a section of the solid pine hewn from one of the trees on this very property.

"Yeah. I couldn't bring myself to part with that. Besides, the designer insisted it added a touch of authenticity."

"Not to mention it was Grandpa's pride and joy." Thank goodness some memories were intact. "It smells heavenly in here." Carla swivelled to face the six-foot tall Christmas tree in the corner. "Is there anything more Christmassy than the smell of fresh pine? These tree ornaments are beautiful." She bit her lip. "Did you keep any of the old stuff?" Grandma's quilt, their baby ornaments…

"Of course. They're all in a closet. I knew you'd be soppy about that stuff."

Carla exhaled. "Well, some of it's pretty special. A few of those ornaments were family heirloom pieces."

"I know." Alexis fingered a sparkly, silver snowflake hanging on the tree. "You have to admit, these are a huge improvement over the awful popsicle stick snowflakes we used to make at school."

Carla's breath caught in her throat. She made those same cheesy snowflakes five years ago with Rhys, right over there where the hand-me-down coffee table used to sit. She blinked back moisture from her eyes.

"I can't believe Mom let us wreck the family tree with our homemade junk." Alexis cringed. "This here is what it's all about." She admired the tree of perfection with pure adoration in her blue eyes.

"Oh, come on. You know Mom treasured everything we made." Carla leaned against one of the love seats and stroked a fur blanket as if it were a cat. "She was super sentimental." *I'm not the only one who's going to be heartbroken if any of our childhood memories have been thrown away.*

Alexis huffed. "So sentimental that she and Dad hightailed it back to the mission field as soon as you left for university."

"Alexis…"

"I'm only saying it how it is. They've been back here a handful of times since. Expected me to keep up the maintenance of this place in case they decide to come back permanently."

"You?" Carla stifled a chuckle at the thought of her sister shoveling the driveway or winterizing the pipes.

"Well, I arrange it. I've rented it out in season and made sure the maintenance guy and housekeeper are both paid." She folded her arms across her chest. "Talking of whom, I hope she put in her full work hours this morning before wandering off downtown."

"Who?"

"That girl I almost ran over."

"Oh. She's the cleaner?" Carla surveyed the immaculate space. "Well, it looks pretty great to me. Honestly, I was kind of bummed that you'd gone ahead and made changes after I spent months on this place before I left." She smiled in an attempt to take the sting out of her words. "How am I supposed to be mad when I get to stay here?" She peeled off her wool jacket and unwound her scarf, setting both down on the back of the loveseat. "It's even warm here now—that's a first. I guess that old fireplace never quite managed to heat the whole cabin."

"Not a problem anymore. Wait until you see the kitchen. It's fully stocked with all your favorite goodies."

"Really?" Sometimes, Alexis showed her heart of gold in all its glory.

Carla followed her around the L-shaped great room into the kitchen. "You have *got* to be kidding me." Carla ran her fingers over a long, smooth, white island that separated the two areas.

A row of sleek, black stools was tucked underneath, and three oversized, black pendants hung above the island. Crisp white cabinetry popped against the warm wooden-planked ceiling and brushed-gold fixtures gleamed elegance and charm.

"Everything is stunning." Carla turned a knob on the state-of-the-art stove. "It's quite the transformation. I'm pretty sure those previous appliances were older than Grandma. That ancient oven took some persuading, and the only one who could really get it to work was…" An image of Rhys cooking dinner popped into her mind, but she couldn't bring herself to finish the sentence.

"Rhys?"

Carla spun around and watched Alexis check the pendants for dust.

"He was a jerk leaving you, but the man sure knew his way around a kitchen." Alexis shed her coat and folded it onto one of the stools.

Carla turned back to the kettle. She lifted it from the hob. Empty. Taking a few slow breaths, she filled the kettle from the golden goose-necked faucet, set it on the burner, and switched on the stove. With the most neutral expression she could muster, she padded over to the island. "Tea?"

"Sounds good. But what aren't you telling me? I know that look. Please don't say you're still pining over that man."

Carla pushed her glasses higher up her face. "He's coming here."

"Who's coming where?" Alexis opened a cabinet and pulled out a box of assorted teas.

"Rhys." Carla licked her dry lips. "He's meeting me here. In the cabin. This evening."

Alexis slammed the box onto the counter. "Excuse me? The guy who smashed your heart into a thousand shards on Christmas Eve and disappeared from your life for five years is back on the scene? Are you crazy? Since when?"

"I know it's a lot." Carla pulled out a stool and sat. "I knew you'd react like this."

Alexis squinted. "Because I'm the one who had to pick up all said shards—"

"Will you at least let me try to explain?" Carla patted the seat next to her, and Alexis stomped around the island to the adjacent stool. "It's kind of a coincidence. Although, I have to believe God had a hand in this."

"Oh, *please* don't pull the God card out of the bag. I had my fill growing up."

Carla's heart ached at her sister's resistance to the mere hint of God, but she squared her shoulders. "I've mentioned the big Christmas fundraising party Madison and Luke have held in Seattle the past couple of years, right?"

"Since the charming missionary met his princess who is exceedingly rich, yes, you've mentioned it. You invited me to the swanky event, remember?"

"Yeah, you flat-out refused. But it's a great opportunity for the investors and supporters to hear what's happing at the orphanage. Madison's sister plans the whole thing—she lives in Seattle and has Madison give her the seal of approval once all the arrangements have been made."

"Rhys comes into the equation how. exactly?"

Carla lifted her index finger in the air. "I'm getting there. A couple of weeks ago, I happened to be in the living room at the orphanage when Madison was checking an email with all the details for the party. The kids were in bed, and I had my head in a book—"

"Surprise, surprise."

"Exactly. I was only half-listening as she was reading the menu out loud. It all sounded delicious, and I was starting to feel hungry listening to the descriptions, and then she got to the dessert." Carla took a deep breath. "It was sugarplum snowflakes."

"Whoa."

"I know. Rhys's signature Christmas dessert he created in this very kitchen." She surveyed the room and pictured him at the ancient oven, tea towel tossed over one shoulder, that lazy smile curving his lips. "Before it was fancy."

Alexis drummed her wine-colored fingernails on the countertop. "So, what did you do?"

"Honestly, I felt sick to my stomach. I checked out the email and went to his website to make sure it was him. *Templeton Eats*. That's the name of his business in Seattle. It was Rhys alright. I hadn't thought about him in forever. Presumed he'd started a life elsewhere, and we'd never run into each other again. Especially with me being in Mexico. It's been a long time…"

Silence filled the kitchen until the kettle whistled.

Carla stood and busied herself making tea to avoid her sister's glare. "Chocolate peppermint still your favorite?" She found white chunky mugs on the open shelves and grabbed the box of teas.

"Sure. So, did you email him or call or what? I want all the details. This is the most excitement you've had in years, even if it's surrounding that lowlife."

Carla dumped two tea bags into the mugs, poured boiling water into each one, and carried them over to the island.

Alexis crossed her legs. "Please tell me you weren't sweet and nice."

Carla lifted her chin. "I slept on it for a night. Or rather didn't sleep at all. I told Madison it was an ex-boyfriend, and she offered to go with a different caterer when she realized it was the same one who broke my heart. We'd spoken about the breakup a bit when she first came to Mexico. Then I thought perhaps this was all meant to be. I'd already booked my flight to come back for Christmas and worked myself up for facing… the past… here at the cabin. Why not get some answers from Rhys at the same time? I was thinking I'd meet him in Seattle after the party, but he offered to come here for a few days. He still has a couple of buddies in town, and one has a vacation rental. That's where he's staying now."

Alexis cupped a steaming mug in her hands and blew on it. "So, he lives back in Seattle again. Gone back home with his tail between his legs, no doubt. Have you spoken on the phone?" She sipped her tea and set it back down.

Carla shook her head and narrowed her eyes. "I didn't like the idea of that. We've kept it to texting. I told him I wasn't on socials, and he's not into it, either, other than his business marketing. Talking on the phone seemed too… intimate. Apparently, he's been in Seattle for a couple of years after being in Europe. He started this catering company, and it sounds like he's busy and happy. Wants to make amends. Said it was important to him that we finally clear the air."

"Is he single?"

"He hasn't mentioned anything about being married. He doesn't have any personal info on his website." His ring finger was bare in all the online photos she'd found.

Alexis pursed her lips, and in that instant, she was a mirror image of their mother. "Be careful."

"I will. I don't want to be naïve, but he sounds genuinely sorry." She lifted a shoulder. "I need to forgive him verbally. For me to move on, as well as for him."

"You've always been a soft touch. Will you tell him"—a muscle twitched in Alexis's cheek—"you know, everything?"

Carla took a moment as she picked up her tea and took a sip of the chocolatey sweetness. "I'm playing it by ear, but I think so." Oh, how she wished she didn't have to. Her hands trembled, and she put the mug back on the island counter. "I guess it depends on how it goes when we first meet. It's going to be hard, even seeing him again. He wants to try to explain his reasons for taking off the way he did. If he wants to come clean and tell me everything from his perspective, then I need to tell him my version of events." She sucked in a breath. "I know you and God aren't tight, but my faith is still really important to me." Tears pooled, and she blinked them away. "I've been praying like crazy about all of this. The forgiveness. The coming back home. The moving on. Plus, I want to be honest with Rhys."

"You're brave, little sister." Alexis reached over and squeezed her hand. "I haven't told you that enough. But you are. Coming here over Christmas wasn't easy.

I'm glad you're ready to get on with your life." She snorted. "Even if it's with a bunch of kids across the globe."

"Actually, that's something else I've been praying about." Carla curled her fingers around the handle of her warm mug. "My next step. Whether it's time to settle down somewhere."

"For real?" Alexis grinned like she'd won the lottery. "Would you come back to Hollybrook?"

Carla inhaled the festive mix of peppermint mingled with fresh pine and felt her shoulders relax. "I need a real home. I miss a home. I love the kids at the orphanage, but I've already been there longer than I originally planned. It feels like I'm marking time. Waiting for something. Plus seeing Luke and Madison so happily married—"

"You want to fall in love and have a family of your own?" Alexis furrowed her brow.

Alexis didn't understand Carla's love for God and children and living abroad—things Carla must have inherited from their missionary parents—but they had shared everything else as they grew up together. Dreams, ambitions, crushes. They might have grown apart over the years, but nothing could change their childhood. Those early years had been simple and happy. If only life could have stayed that way.

"Sure, I want to get married and have kids, but I need to find my sense of place first." Butterflies shifted in her belly. "Alexis, what if I came back and lived *here*?" She took in the exquisite home that also held so many treasured memories in her heart.

Alexis stood. "Here? In the cabin?" She looked as if she'd been slapped. "After what happened?"

Carla glanced at the back door and shuddered. She'd deal with that later. Another sip of hot tea settled her stomach. "I didn't expect to feel this way. I've been dreading coming back." A beam of sunlight chose that moment to pierce through the kitchen window and warm her cheek. "But it feels so different now with all the changes. Different in a positive, healthy way. It seems light and bright and airy and fresh. I kind of imagined it would feel claustrophobic and dark. That I would need to get out as soon as possible." She walked over to a love seat with her tea and settled into the buttery soft cushions. "Now, I might just want to stay forever."

Carla's chuckle fell flat when Alexis came and sat next to her. "You've got your serious-big-sister face on. What is it?"

"The thing is, I didn't do all these renos for the fun of it. Or even to up the rental rates." She tucked her hair behind her ears. "I'm sorry, but it's not going to be our property any longer."

Carla's mouth fell open as her childhood memories and future dreams dissolved into a puddle of melted snow. "How do you mean?"

Alexis tilted her head. "We're selling the cabin."

Chapter Three

CARLA'S HEART SANK AS SHE SET her mug on the coffee table. This was the only place that felt like home. "Excuse me? Selling the cabin?" She shook her head in confusion. For a moment, she felt sure God was tugging her heartstrings to stay. "Why? Do Mom and Dad know?"

"Of course, they know. They're coming back from India less and less, and when they do visit, they stay at my place so they get to spend time with me. It makes sense all around to sell."

"When is it going on the market?"

Alexis folded her arms across her chest. "It's just been listed. I'm not expecting any action over Christmas, and I'm waiting until after you leave to put up a sign."

The thudding of Carla's heartbeat reminded her of the hammering of nails she had put her efforts into with her meager renovations of this place five years ago. The railings replaced on the porch. Mantel varnished. Holes filled. Floors scrubbed. Her pulse raced as she realized time was running out and there was not a single thing she could do about that. "But it could be snapped up anytime?"

"It could. Yes."

Carla stood and paced the refinished floorboards. "Grandpa built this home with his own two hands. We can't just let it go."

"Oh, trust me, we aren't just letting it go." She smirked. "The market is ripe for the picking, and with the remodeling, we'll make an absolute killing."

"It's about *money*?" Carla planted a hand on one hip. "What about family? Home?" She gestured toward Grandpa's mantel. "A sense of history and belonging?"

Alexis drew herself to full height, towering over Carla. "Says she who took off to Mexico and left *me* to deal with the cabin."

"I thought you wanted that. You're a realtor. I thought you enjoyed bossing everyone around with the maintenance and renting and stuff." She cocked her head to one side. "Why didn't you stay in Vancouver after university anyway? Why come back here where it's sleepy and comfortable and very *not* you?"

"Because I like being the big fish in the little lake." Alexis flicked her long hair over one shoulder, retrieved her coat from the stool, and slid into it with grace and poise. "I like people looking up to me and asking me for advice. I like that I'm successful. I like going on vacation to exotic locations and visiting you in Mexico and my parents in India whenever I want. So, there you have it. I'm selfish." She slipped her phone from her coat pocket and checked the screen. "I'm also keenly aware our parents need money to survive in their old age, wherever they choose to spend it. One of us has to figure that out." She shoved the phone back in her pocket and fastened her buttons with more force than necessary. "I'm guessing it's not going to be you?"

Wow. "Oh, Lex, I'm sorry." Carla closed the chasm between them and hugged her big sister tight. "You're not selfish. I'm the selfish one." She spoke into the shoulder of the navy coat. "You're the glue that keeps this family together."

After several awkward seconds, Alexis's stiff arms softened, and she reciprocated the hug.

Carla continued, "I've been off-grid, and I expected everything to work out like magic. When I saw how perfect this cabin is now…"

Alexis pulled back and held her at arm's length. "I guess I did too good a job. I didn't expect you to fall in love with it like that. I wanted it to be easier for you to be here than it was last time. Different. Clean. You know what I mean? I wanted your final stay in the cabin to be fabulous."

Carla nodded. "It will be. You've seen to that. Madison will be blown away after the way I described our rustic home-away-from-home." She managed a smile.

"You're not mad with me? You know I'm a businesswoman."

"I'm sad. Not mad. I'm not going to brood and ruin the time I have here. It really is beautiful."

"Wait until you see the clawfoot tub in the bathroom." Alexis winked.

Carla gasped. "No way. Well, once I've had my conversation with Rhys, I know exactly where I'll be heading."

"Hey, I can come back after I've walked Lily and answered some work calls, if you like. I can wait until Rhys leaves to give you some privacy, but I didn't expect you to spend a night all alone up here." Alexis's phone chirped, and she took it back out and tapped a quick message. "I mean, don't be a martyr. Gosh, Carla, the last time you were here…"

"No, I'll be fine." Carla leaned over to her coat on the love seat and plucked out her own phone. "I have reception, and I promise to call if I get freaked out.

Besides, I'm not totally on my own up here." She nodded toward the front window. "Seems some of these other homes around the lake are occupied."

"True. There are about fifteen properties out there now, and I'm pretty sure they're all lived in year-round. I'm not going to lie, though, I wish you had a vehicle."

"Madison's renting a car when she arrives. She didn't mind and that way she can pick up Luke from the airport on Christmas Eve."

"This is going to be a whirlwind of a trip. Sure you have time to squeeze in a few hours with me?" Alexis gave her puppy-dog eyes.

"Are you telling me you're not going to be working at all for the next few days?" She glowered at the chirping phone in her sister's hand and slid her own into her jeans pocket.

"I may have a few clients needing my attention, but I promise I'll be all done by Christmas Day. We're still spending it here, aren't we?"

"Absolutely." Carla eyed the elegant Christmas tree. "We'll have a special breakfast with Luke and Madison, and then they'll leave for Seattle, and we can have the rest of the day to ourselves."

The last Christmas at the cabin. Ever. A sigh escaped her lips.

"Then you'll head to Seattle on Boxing Day?"

As they walked toward the entrance, Carla couldn't resist running her hand over the love seat's fur throw again. "Right. The fundraising party. You know you're invited. You can still change your mind and tag along. It's going to be super fancy. Could be good for your schmoozing..."

Alexis dug into her designer purse. "I'll think about it." She dropped a key into Carla's hand. "I have another but try not to lose this one. Make sure you lock up even if you go for a walk around the lake." She blanched. "I guess I don't need to tell you to be careful up here."

"You don't. But I will." Carla raised her chin and squeezed the key in her balled-up fist. "I need to do this myself. But thank you. Promise I'll give you a shout later." She opened the front door, and a swoosh of cold air blasted her face. "I'm glad you kept the door blue."

"I couldn't imagine it any other way. It's good for some things not to change, right?"

"Right." Carla squeezed her sister's hand. "Drive safe."

"Call me. I'd like to know how it goes with Rhys." Alexis's forehead creased. "For your sake, I hope it doesn't unearth too much pain."

"I'll be all right. Thanks again for bringing me home." *Home.* Even if she could only enjoy the cabin as such for a few more days.

Carla watched Alexis drive away in the truck, locked the door, and glared at her suitcase at the bottom of the stairs. She should unpack and settle in while she still had the energy. The red eye from Manzanillo with a lengthy layover in Seattle would hit her hard by the end of the day. Hopefully, exhaustion would kick in *after* she'd spoken with Rhys.

She had to be on her game for that particular conversation.

With a struggle, she lifted her case up the stairs to her bedroom. The master bedroom. She'd spent many happy hours reading here that last winter before she left for Mexico. Claiming this space as her own had been such a treat after sharing the smaller bedroom with her sister during their growing up years. Now, the room had been refreshed with twinkling white lights and emanated a familiar charm and warmth from the gray rug covering the floor to the airy wooden vaulted ceilings.

Carla heaved her case on top of the new creamy bedding and crossed the room to the window where matching curtains hung beside the addition of a cream leather armchair. She wrapped her arms around herself and took in the rear of the property. To the right, the area was clear of trees. Beneath the snow was probably still lawn. She'd been given the task of mowing the grass for years. Just out of sight to the left was the oval-shaped lake, and then directly behind the cabin lay a clump of tall pine trees that led to one of several hiking trails. She'd shown Rhys all the trails and nature hikes and had even persuaded him to snowshoe straight out from the cabin. Her chest tightened. He left without warning. Not knowing what would happen to her next.

She stepped closer to the window, pressed her fingers on the chilled glass, and peered down at the back porch. It was covered, but she could picture the wooden slats. Hear the creak of the back door. Feel the blood leave her face…

Ping.

Relieved the memory was cut short, she pulled her phone from her jeans. Madison.

HI, CARLA! CHECKING IN TO MAKE SURE YOU MADE IT HOME OKAY. ALSO TO LET YOU KNOW I'LL BE PRAYING FOR YOU THIS EVENING WHEN YOU MEET RHYS. THE KIDS ALL SAY HOLA, AND I HAVE STRICT INSTRUCTIONS TO GIVE YOU HUGS FROM EACH ONE OF THEM WHEN I ARRIVE. I MISS THEM ALREADY, AND I'M NOT EVEN AT THE AIRPORT YET! SEE YOU TOMORROW.

Carla closed her eyes. Every time she considered moving on from the orphanage, she missed the faces of those beautiful children and her friendship with both Luke and Madison. Saying goodbye to them all would be heartbreaking. She hoped for clarity with this "coming home" trip, but so far, she'd been wooed by the beauty of the refreshed cabin only to be devastated by the revelation that it was being sold.

One step at a time.

She thanked Madison, slipped her phone away, and decided to check out the other rooms. She poked her head into the smaller bedroom, where two double beds took up most of the space. A delightful mix of rustic and contemporary was accented with stylish lamps against a color scheme of forest green and fresh white. Luke and Madison would be more than comfortable here.

Then down the hallway, she entered the shared white-on-white bathroom… wow. Generous in size, the room still held a tiled shower along the far wall, along with double vanity and toilet area, but the clawfoot tub stole the show as its gleaming feet and faucet caught the afternoon sun streaming down through the skylight. Carla perched on the edge of the bath and made herself a promise. *Later.* She inspected several expensive-looking bottles of lotions and potions and selected a perfect lavender bubble bath. *I could get used to this. But I won't.*

Her stomach gurgled a reminder that she should eat before Rhys arrived, so she left her spa thoughts behind and padded downstairs. She had three hours. Plenty of time. Alexis had said there was food stocked in the cupboards.

As she rounded the corner into the living room and caught a glimpse of the back door, nausea roiled. She hesitated. No. She couldn't put off the dreaded moment any longer. She had to revisit the exact spot where her nightmare had become a reality.

God, I know You're here with me. I think I'm probably being ridiculous, but I have to open that door. Stand on the porch. Claim it as the place of peace I used to love. Would You help me, please?

Before she could talk herself out of her actions, Carla took long strides through the living room, passed the stunning Christmas tree, and touched the back-door knob. The key was in the lock, so she turned it in one robotic motion and opened the door wide—and gasped.

Whatever she was expecting, this area exceeded her wildest imagination. The porch was almost an extension of the transformed living room, illuminated by strands of twinkling white lights. She stepped outside, allowed her clenched fists to open, and breathed deep and slow, allowing every cell in her body to drink in the surreal warmth of the space. With a pressing need to speak to her sister, she pulled the phone from her jeans.

"Alexis?"

"Hey, I just got home. Everything all right there? Do I need to come back?"

"No. Everything's great." The charming, decorated Christmas tree sitting between the cute wooden rocking chairs brought tears to her eyes, and her bottom lip trembled. This was not what she expected. "I'm on the back porch and, well, I don't know what to say other than thank you."

"You like it?"

She closed the door behind her and collapsed onto the new wicker love seat next to a pile of cozy blankets. Words lodged in her throat as she touched the soft fleece throws. "You have no idea how much this means to me. I've been working myself up to come back out here again after what happened. I thought it would feel… the same. It doesn't." She chuckled. "I can't explain. I opened the door, and it felt like God Himself invited me onto the porch. The sun's shining, and I don't even feel the cold. There's this warm breeze."

"I may not be able to take the credit for all that." Lily's bark sounded in the background.

"I know, but it's charming and welcoming and—not at all how I remember it."

"Good. That was my plan." The smile in Alexis's voice was obvious. "Some renos were for resale and some were especially for you to enjoy."

"I'm a mess here." Carla sniffled and laughed at the same time. "Seriously, it was so kind of you. It's bolstered my confidence to speak with Rhys about everything, too." She wiped tears from her cold face with the back of her hand. "I should go inside. I didn't think to put on a jacket." She stood and retreated to the living room, careful to lock the back door behind her.

"Is he going to be there soon?"

"I have time to eat and unpack, but I'm ready. If you think of it, say a prayer for me?"

A grunt. "Fine."

Rhys Templeton sat at his favorite table in Angel Cakes bakery and inhaled the familiar comfort of sugary cinnamon lingering in the air. His flight from Seattle had arrived first thing that morning, and after settling in at his friend's place, he'd spent most of the day walking and getting reacquainted with the town. A lifetime ago, he'd spent almost a year here, working at this very bakery and falling in love with Carla James.

From his spot at the window, he watched everyday people doing regular things in Hollybrook. Days before Christmas, most seemed laser focused, and the cold temperatures ushered shoppers inside to warm up as they likely purchased their last minute gifts.

Should he have bought something for Carla? No, that would be too much. The fact that she even agreed to talk to him was a miracle, let alone meet him face-to-face. The last thing he wanted to do was let her presume he thought he could make everything right with a present.

"Here's your coffee, Rhys." Molly placed a steaming oversized cup and saucer topped with some impressive latte art onto the table.

"Fancy." He grinned at the woman who had been more like a mother to him than his own.

"Don't be too impressed. I can only actually do a heart. It took me over a hundred attempts to master it when we first got the machine." She buried her worn, wrinkled hands in her apron pockets. "It's what the people want these days."

"Business busy as ever?" He took a sip. Delicious.

She nodded, her shiny gray bob dancing on her shoulders. "Especially this time of year. You want to sample my latest creation?"

"Have I ever said no to your baking, Molly?"

"Be right back." Her kind eyes crinkled, and she bustled off to the counter.

Rhys leaned forward and rested his elbows on the scarred pine table. Carla had spent hours at this very spot with her book stack. She would come from the library and read while he worked for Molly as her right-hand man. He'd considered specializing as a pastry chef at one point, but the pull of restaurant life in France with its coq au vin and boeuf bourguignon had been too tempting.

"Here you go. Peppermint chocolate shortbread with candy cane drizzle. Be honest, now." Molly stood and watched, hands on her ample hips.

Rhys ate with his eyes first as he studied the stunning morsel. He could already tell the shortbread would be rich yet light. Not too sweet. The drizzle was studded with tiny shards of candy cane, a delightful touch.

He lifted the rectangle and took a bite, closing his eyes to fully enjoy the experience.

"Molly." He licked his lips, the infusion of peppermint soothing and festive. "You've done it again. I learned from the best. It's phenomenal."

Her complexion pinked up, and she squeezed his arm. "You think so? That means an awful lot coming from a professional French chef like you."

"I know so." He kissed both her cheeks, just as he'd learned in France. "I'm not exactly a French chef." He laughed. "I think real French chefs might have something to say about that, but they taught me a thing or two. Almost as much as you did." He gave her a wink.

"Go on with you." She chuckled and collected empty mugs from a nearby table. "Well, I, for one, am thrilled to see you again."

"Really? I was in a bad place back then."

"You had your reasons. I always knew you had a good heart. That you would make something of yourself eventually."

"I guess being the man of the house in elementary school back in Seattle gave me a solid work ethic, if nothing else." His jaw popped at the memories of his mom, broken and bruised, a slave to addictions beyond his young comprehension.

"Whatever else happened is in the past, you're here now. I know things didn't work out with our lovely Carla James, but you'll always be welcome at Angel Cakes. You come and visit whenever you like."

"Thanks, Molly." He bit into the shortbread and nodded. "I hope Carla feels the same way."

"I heard she was coming home for Christmas. That sister of hers ordered some special desserts for the holidays and said she was visiting." She held the mugs to her chest. "Oh, dear boy. Are you going to see her? Do you think there's any chance of you and Carla—"

"We're having a conversation. Clearing the air. Making amends. Well, I am. I have a lot to be sorry about, and she's been gracious enough to agree to hear me out. That's all. So, don't start the rumor mill rolling. Please?"

"Me? Of course not, but I'll be praying. You were the perfect couple."

"Then pray she can forgive me. That's what I'm praying for more than anything."

Molly raised a penciled-in brow. "Are you and God friends again? You had a rough patch for a while there."

He scratched his stubbly chin. More like a storm of epic proportions that took him to hell and back. "Things had to get worse before they got better, but yes. We're friends, to say the least." He now had a real relationship with a Father who loved him. Someone he could trust and depend on always.

"Glad to hear that, Rhys Templeton. About time you smartened up." She ruffled his hair on her way back to the counter.

So many fond memories in this bakery. In Hollybrook. With Carla.

So much of his future hinged on their meeting tonight.

Chapter Four

CARLA GLANCED AT HER PHONE. AGAIN. Rhys would be arriving any minute. She checked her hair in the bathroom mirror and smoothed the soft waves that flowed almost to her waist. Had she applied a little more makeup than usual? Maybe. Who was she kidding? At the orphanage, she wore zero makeup and tied her hair up in a messy bun most days. But this wasn't most days. Not that she had anything to prove, but meeting her ex-boyfriend, after not seeing him in the flesh for five years, was a big deal. Had he changed much? Had she? Would he kick himself for letting her go?

The "effortless chic" look was taking a great deal of effort and not much chic was happening, but at least her skinny jeans and black chunky-knit cropped sweater emitted the right vibe. The trendy tortoiseshell glasses always gave her confidence a boost. Glasses were her one extravagance, and she had a pair to fit pretty much every mood and occasion. If she had to wear specs, they might as well make a statement. A final spritz of the subtle orange blossom perfume she always wore, and she was done.

6:59 PM

She heard a vehicle pull up outside above the soft strains of Christmas music playing on repeat. *Showtime.*

One deep breath and she sauntered down the stairs as casually as her racing heart would allow. Curtains were drawn. Welcoming porch lights on. *Let him knock on the door. Be cool.*

A familiar *knock-knock-knock* and her pulse quickened. She stood at the door and collected every ounce of calm she could muster before swinging it open.

"Hi, Rhys."

There he was. On her doorstep. The past five years seemed to evaporate into the snowflakes that drifted on the inky night sky as those hazel eyes opened wide, and he attempted a smile.

"I didn't know if I should bring anything, so I made fudge." Rhys thrust a small brown box tied with twine toward her. "Chocolate orange."

"Thanks." He always made the best fudge. This flavor was new. What else was new with the man she once considered her soulmate? Carla swallowed her nerves and forced her hands to receive the box. "That was thoughtful. Come on in."

She moved back and made space for him to kick off his boots and hang his jacket on the coat stand. "I see it's snowing again."

"Yeah." A grin filled his face. "It's awesome."

"You always did love the snow."

"We both did. You know I'm a big kid. I can't help it."

No, he was no kid. He was a full-grown man, and even more handsome than she remembered. "Why don't you take a look around? I hope you're prepared for the ultimate fixer-upper reveal."

He whistled his appreciation as he walked through the living area. "Wow. Your sister sure pulled out all the stops with the remodeling here."

"I know. At first it stung a little when I thought of the months it took you and me to get it into decent shape. I couldn't stay mad long. It really is stunning. Check out the kitchen."

He followed her into the space. "It's phenomenal."

"I thought you'd appreciate it." She put the fudge box on the island, headed over to the hob, and then turned back. "Tea? Hot chocolate?" She lifted the kettle. "Unless you want wine—there's some in the fridge."

"Umm, hot chocolate sounds great, thanks." He ran his hand across the countertops and inspected the fancy bread maker and espresso machine. "No expense spared. I like it."

She switched on the burner, grabbed a couple of mugs, and located the hot chocolate canister while he pulled out a stool, scraping the wooden floor.

"Carla, I know this is super awkward, but I want to thank you for even agreeing to meet up with me. After what I did…"

So, they were diving straight in. Carla took a deep breath as she came around the island and joined him on another stool.

He threaded his fingers through his thick mop of sandy-colored hair. A shade darker than Carla remembered. "I don't quite know where to begin."

"It's okay. I'm sure we've both got a lot to say, but enough time has passed that I think it can be amicable." She measured her words, determined to not break down in front of him.

"Thanks." His shoulders relaxed.

"I'm not mad, Rhys. Five years is a long time. I believe God orchestrated this"—she waved her hand between them—"meeting of ours to happen. The timing was good."

"How so?" His eyes widened.

"I haven't been back to Hollybrook since I left five years ago." She pressed a hand against her stomach. "I've been waiting for it to feel… right." A deep breath.

"This Christmas, it just did. I don't think it was an accident that Madison's sister booked you to cater our fundraising party. What are the chances?"

He nodded. "That was wild. Your email was also a surprise, to say the least." He licked his lips. "Like I said, I need to ask for your forgiveness for what happened. To try to explain. Even if it was ages ago. I need to make amends. Not only because it's part of my program—"

The kettle blew out a demanding whistle from the stove. "Program?" Carla slid from the stool. "Hang on, let me get our drinks." She scurried off and made quick work of two hot chocolates. What program was he talking about? She carried the mugs back and placed them on the island. "You were saying?"

"Yeah. My program. AA. Alcoholics Anonymous." His face reddened. "Hence the preference for hot chocolate over wine."

"Oh." Didn't see that coming. She closed her gaping mouth. "Care to elaborate?"

Rhys untied the twine on the fudge box as he spoke. "I needed help, Carla. When we were together, I was well and truly down the slippery slope of alcohol abuse."

What? She cocked her head to one side. "You were? How could I not have known? We enjoyed a glass of wine together with dinner and maybe on occasion by the fire in the evening, but I don't recall it getting out of hand. I don't think I ever saw you drunk."

She went to pick up her hot chocolate to give her a moment to take in this news and realized she'd forgotten whipped cream. "Cream?"

"Please."

She hopped down and retrieved a can from the fridge. As she swirled a generous amount into each mug, a memory of them having a whipped cream spray fight played out in the recesses of her mind. She glanced at Rhys, and he gave a half-smile. Was he recalling the same moment that occurred mere days before he left? She stowed the can and joined him again.

Rhys cleared his throat and took a sip of his drink, licking a layer of cream from his top lip. "Anyway. To answer your question, alcoholics can be very adept at hiding the truth. Covering our tracks. Keeping secrets. Carrying the strongest breath mints. I made it my goal to never over-drink in front of you. What you didn't see was the way I grabbed the bottle on my nightstand before I did anything else first thing in the morning." He blinked up at the ceiling. "Or the flask I kept filled in my truck to top up as needed through the day. Or the nightcap I treated myself to after I said goodnight to you and collapsed into my bed night after night." He bowed his head and studied the mug he cradled in his lap.

"Silent Night" played in the background, and Carla couldn't for the life of her think what to say. Had their relationship been based on lies? Would he be trustworthy now? Ever? Their own silence stretched out between them.

"Carla, I'm sorry. For lying to you. For breaking your heart. For leaving without the guts to explain why. For everything." He placed the mug back on the counter and looked up at her with the most sorrow-filled eyes she'd ever seen. "Can you forgive me?"

She reached out and clasped his hands out of old habit. They were rougher. Hardened. What had he been through to get to the other side of this? Her heart squeezed, but she had already worked through her forgiveness and prayed about her response to him in person. If anything, his actions made a little more sense now. "Yes. I forgive you, Rhys."

"Really?" His voice broke, and tears filled his eyes.

She nodded and released his hands, suddenly self-conscious. "Before you go thinking I'm some kind of saint who can forgive at the drop of a hat, I'll remind you I've had years to work through what happened that Christmas Eve. I went to see a counsellor in Mexico. I've had great support from Alexis, from friends, from my church family."

"Your parents, too? How are they, anyway?"

She shrugged. "They're well. Still in India. They're always on the other end of the phone when I need them." Not that a phone call did much to soothe her soul. "I couldn't have handled it as well as I did without God's strength. He's been my anchor through… everything." She eyed the back door, and her skin prickled.

"I remember your special Bible verse, you know." He grabbed the length of twine from the fudge box and twirled it between his fingers.

"You do?"

"Sure. Deuteronomy 31:8." He closed his eyes, and a line formed between his eyebrows. "'The Lord himself goes before you and will be with you; he will never leave you nor forsake you. Do not be afraid; do not be discouraged.'"

Words she'd clung to like a life raft in a raging storm. He had no idea. Carla pursed her lips. "Impressive memory."

"After I left, I prayed you would hold it close. Believe it. It sounds like you did." Rhys leaned one elbow on the counter. "I apologize for leaving with no explanation. For causing you pain and worry." He furrowed his brow. "I guess in my ignorance I hoped you would get over me quickly and find someone worthy of your… goodness."

"My *goodness*?"

He shrugged. "You were always such a rock solid Christian. I knew I would drag you down. I had to deal with my own demons and let you go and do your missionary thing. I could tell you were second guessing your decision to go to Mexico. I didn't want to hold you back."

She would have stayed here with him in a heartbeat, but she still had questions. Carla took her mug and cupped it in her hands. The warmth gave her courage to keep asking details she'd been dying to know for way too long.

"So where did you go? After you… broke up with me?" She tried not to sound snippy, but even though she forgave him, the reality still stung, and being here was bringing back all manner of heartache. She had a long way to go on this journey and no number of renovations, twinkly lights, or fudge would make the remnants of pain disappear like magic. She took a long sip of her hot chocolate. "You always dreamed of going to Europe to cook. I wondered if that's what you did."

"Actually, yes, but it was nowhere near as romantic as the ideals I used to dream up. I cashed in all my savings, told my family in Seattle that I would be off-grid for the foreseeable future—which they didn't blink an eye about—and found a cheap flight to France."

His dysfunctional family had always been a disappointment to him. Addictions had been an issue for his mom. Was a need for this type of dependency in his genes? Perhaps abusing alcohol was a result of that family stress and made him want to escape reality. Maybe going to France was part of that escape, too.

"How did you survive over in France? You spoke pretty good French, but how does someone start from scratch in a new country? Did you even have a visa?"

"It's a long story, but I wasn't exactly on the up-and-up legally speaking. I even slept on the streets a few nights at the beginning." He winced. "It was rough. I took whatever work I could find in kitchens, but I managed to drink away most of my measly pay. It was far from glamorous. Imagine washing dishes for hours on end for abusive bosses who knew they could get me to work for next to nothing because I was completely desperate."

Carla blew out a quick breath. "It sounds horrific. But things obviously improved for you to be here now with your own catering company in Seattle." She savored another gulp of her drink.

He pulled a leather wallet from his jeans. "This guy here saved my life." He shared a tattered photograph of a middle-aged rotund man in chef whites. "Chef Paul. He saw me hanging around outside a church one Sunday night—I was still trying to work on my relationship with God—and this guy gave me a challenge. Said he would take me under his wing and give me work in his restaurant kitchen if I did my part by stopping with the drinking. Apparently, I reminded him of his brother who was an alcoholic. He'd never been able to help him."

Carla studied the kind eyes of this Chef Paul before handing back the treasured photograph. "So, he was your guardian angel."

Rhys chuckled. "I wouldn't call him an angel exactly. He was a hard taskmaster, but he loved God and wanted to help me out. Became my spiritual mentor, my accountability partner, and my best friend. Helped me dry out, shape up, and get my act together. He also taught me to cook. Over the years, I worked crazy hard and earned a good reputation on the outskirts of Paris. Then, when the time was right, I came back to Seattle."

"That's amazing." Carla drained the last of her drink. "You've come a long way."

"Thanks. I'm still such a work in progress. Especially with the alcohol issues. I rely on God every single day to get me through. Sometimes hour by hour."

"I'm pretty sure that's the way it's supposed to be for us all."

"Maybe. But I feel like I've seen the bottom of the proverbial barrel, you know? It's ugly. Empty. I don't ever want to go there again." The lines in his forehead were deeper than before.

Perhaps, one day, she'd feel comfortable to ask for details of his life in France. What really happened in those first weeks and months. Or maybe this was as far as they needed to walk down memory lane.

"Hey, it takes guts to come back home. Trust me, I know. And to start your own business? I'm sure it wasn't easy."

Rhys finished his drink and nodded. "I was lucky my uncle in Seattle still wanted to be a part of my life. Remember him?"

"Yeah. He was the only family member you were close to, if I remember correctly. The wealthy uncle."

"And willing to invest in me as a chef and a recovering alcoholic. He's been a tremendous help." He gestured toward the fudge. "These are his favorites." He offered her the opened box. "See what you think. You were always a great guinea pig when it came to my cooking and baking.”

She took a square and popped it in her mouth. “Oh, my word.” She closed her eyes. “I need a moment.” The smooth dark chocolate infused with sweet orange tasted like… Christmas. “This is divine. For the record, I never once minded being your food guinea pig.”

Carla laughed, and he joined in until tears sprang to her eyes. An unexpected well of emotion rose from her chest, and she had the sudden urge to hug him. Would that be weird? Probably. She took a deep breath, blinked back moisture, and jumped down from the stool. She grabbed his empty mug. “Can I get you anything else?”

“No thanks. Well, maybe I’ll take one piece.” He helped himself to the fudge and spoke around it. “I’d love to hear about you, Carla. Tell me about your life. If it’s not too painful, what happened after I left? Did you go straight to Mexico? Meet anyone special?”

His kind smile was a dagger to her heart. He’d dislodged something buried deep inside her, and she knew she had to tell him her story. Would the truth be too much for him to bear after wrestling with demons of his own? Would the guilt eat him alive, or would this be another step they both needed to take in order to move on with their lives?

“Do you want to sit in the living room where it’s a bit warmer?” The fire’s inviting glow would take them farther from the back door, and perhaps she would muster up the courage to share what happened to her on that Christmas Eve after he left her alone and vulnerable.

Broken hearted.

And perfect prey.

Chapter Five

Carla led the way and sank into one of the love seats, gesturing for Rhys to take the other. She tugged a throw over her lap and fiddled with the tassels. Where to begin?

"So, when you suddenly left, it came as a shock, of course." She adjusted her glasses. "I'd planned to spend the whole day with you—a special Christmas Eve." She chanced a look at him.

Rhys leaned in, hands clasped. He wanted to know, and she was going to tell him.

"For the record, I'm grateful we always had boundaries when it came to our relationship." She felt her cheeks heat up, and it had nothing to do with her proximity to the fireplace filling the space between them. "Especially while we fixed up the place, it would have been easy for you to sleep here, and some nights it was so hard seeing you leave. But that last evening when we kissed? I had no clue you were kissing me goodbye." She tucked her hair behind her ears. "Maybe I would have tried to persuade you to stay. For us to work through your issues together. To postpone Mexico. I don't know. Anyway, when I came downstairs on Christmas Eve and found your note…" *I'm so sorry, Carla. I'm leaving to start a new life in Europe. Please don't wait for me.* She blinked at the memory. "I was wrecked. So was Christmas. Has been ever since."

He wiped his hands down his face, and her eye was drawn to his strong jawline, more pronounced in the warm glow of the table lamps. "I'm so sorry. I was such a jerk."

"And a coward." She pulled back her shoulders and pushed the throw aside, heat now coursing through her body as she prepared to share what happened. "With no explanation, I didn't know what to do. I guessed you were safe, but I had no idea exactly where you were heading. Europe's a big place. So, I phoned around, spoke with a couple of friends. You didn't tell a soul."

"I know. I couldn't tell anyone. I cracked, and I needed to disappear." He shook his head, and a lock of hair fell over his eyes. "I was being completely selfish. I didn't stop long enough to consider how that would affect your life or your Christmas. Or every Christmas thereafter."

Lord, give me the words to say here. "It wasn't only a broken heart that affected my Christmas." She took in a shaky breath and glanced over at the back door for a moment. "Something else happened that day. Something horrific. The real reason I haven't been back here at the cabin since."

"What? What happened, Carla?"

His hazel eyes widened, but she dropped her gaze and stared at her hands trembling in her lap. She couldn't look at him for this.

"After I'd cried and phoned my sister, I was sitting here wondering what on earth to do next. In fact, I had my laptop and was scrolling flights to Mexico. Figured I needed to stick with my plan. Any excuse to not think about you. About us." She licked her lips. "When I heard someone on the back porch, I thought you'd come back. Had a change of heart."

She peeked up at his sudden movement and watched him stare at the back door. She grabbed a fur cushion from beside her and clutched it to her chest like a shield. "Obviously, it wasn't you."

He turned back, his face pale.

She lowered her eyes and studied the cushion. "I hurried over to the door, opened it, and rammed straight into the chest of… a man. He had a balaclava covering his face. Black clothes." A shudder ran up her spine. "He slammed his foot inside so I couldn't shut the door. I shrieked. Tried to run past him to get out of the, but he was stronger than me. Bigger. Blocked me outside on the porch. He smelled like winter mints." Her chin wobbled. "He threw me against the furniture we had out back. Hit me." She touched her cheek at the memory and swallowed the boulder in her throat. "And then dragged me back inside by my hair, threw me to the floor, and… and then he was on top of me, so heavy, his hands all over me… I tried to scream. I could barely breathe…"

Rhys let out a strangled gasp. "Oh, dear Lord, no."

Her voice fell to a whisper. "He raped me, Rhys. He raped me." She tasted bile and gave herself a moment. "Then he left. Slammed the door. Disappeared."

She hadn't noticed through the blur of tears that Rhys now knelt before her. His cheeks were wet, too.

He tucked her long hair behind her ears with a tenderness that took her breath away. "I… I'm sorry… so sorry I wasn't there." He held her fingers in his own, head bowed. Was he praying?

"I never found out who he was."

Rhys's head snapped up. "What do you mean? They didn't catch him? Couldn't get an ID on him?"

She shook her head. "I didn't report it."

Rhys sat next to her on the love seat, one arm around her trembling shoulders. "I have no right to ask any questions—but why not?"

Carla took off her glasses and wiped her eyes on her sleeve. "I was a mess. Devastated. My heart was broken, and I'd been attacked. I was undone physically and emotionally. The only ray of hope I had left was the thought of those children in Mexico. They needed me, and I needed them. By the time Alexis arrived, I'd made the decision to swear her to secrecy and that I'd catch an earlier flight to Mexico. Put it all behind me." Although, that had been wishful thinking. The road to healing had taken years of counseling and work on her part.

Rhys stood and plodded over to the back door. "This was my fault. I should've been here." He ran both hands through his hair as he paced. "If only—"

"Don't. Don't do that." Carla walked over to him and touched his arm, the bicep tight beneath his sweater as he stopped and faced her. "Rhys, you couldn't have known what was going to happen." She had dreaded he would blame himself for this. "He could've been watching me for days or weeks—or it could've been the wrong place at the wrong time."

"No. This was a result of yet another of the poor choices I've made in my life." He shook his head and balled his fists. "How can you bear to even meet with me? Talk to me?" His voice cracked, and her heart clenched. "How can you be kind and loving to me, Carla? When this awful thing happened to you?"

"Stop." She held him at arm's length and looked deep into his eyes. "I knew you'd blame yourself— heck, I blamed you, too, for the first while. It was five years ago, and I can assure you, I've had the very best help and counseling to get me through."

He squinted. "How have you coped? How did you get on with your life after that?"

"Like I said before, God has been my rock. You understand. He's there for us whatever life throws our way. Trust me, it hasn't been an easy journey, and I've struggled. *Really* struggled. I've wrestled with whether or not I should tell you about the attack because I don't want you to blame yourself. It was *the attacker's* fault, and his alone." She tilted her head and squeezed his arms. "I have regrets that I didn't press charges and at least attempt to find him. All I knew back then was that I had to leave."

He shrugged. "I'm the expert at regrets. And at leaving."

"Then you understand." Her hands fell to her sides. "Don't get me wrong, I still have nightmares where this monster has gone on to attack other girls. I pray every night that I was a one-off for him. Alexis says there was never news of any similar attacks in the area, so I cling to that. I'm okay."

"Really?" The twinkly white lights from the Christmas tree reflected in his eyes.

She let out a ragged sigh and admitted her current reality. "I'm kind of skittish around men. I have trust issues. Plus those occasional nightmares. Like you, I'm a work in progress."

"Come here, my brave girl." He pulled her into a hug, and she allowed herself to melt into his familiar embrace.

She still fit perfectly. Tremors ran through his body, and she sensed him trying to hold his emotions in check. Would she even want to be *his girl* if she had half the chance again? Was he still a loose cannon or could they settle down together with a new beginning after all these years? *God, my head is so sensible, but my heart is squeezed in a vice-grip here.* She could lose herself in Rhys's love again. To get swept away in this moment, but she needed time to process. Gain clarity on the current racing of her pulse and the sparks reigniting in the pit of her belly.

She stepped back. "Hey, I think it's best if you go now. I'm exhausted, and we've both got a lot to think about."

His face was pale and pinched, as if someone had knocked the stuffing out of him. He eyed the back door again. "Really? Will you be all right? Is your sister coming up here tonight, so you won't be alone?"

She raised her chin. "I'll be okay. I need to do this."

"You sure?"

"Positive."

His hands twitched. "I guess I should go for a drive or a long walk then. I know my triggers and what might send me spiraling to drink." Tears glistened in his eyes. "I came to try to make amends as part of my recovery, and you've been gracious enough to forgive me." He closed the gap between them and kissed the top of her head. "I don't know yet if I can forgive myself." He pulled back and made his way toward the front door.

"Rhys?" Would this be the last time she saw him? Other than the fundraising party in Seattle. Why was her heart breaking? She loved him so long ago. He'd moved on and so had she. Right? "Promise me you'll drive carefully out there?"

"I will."

She followed, grabbed his jacket from the coat rack, and handed it to him.

He slipped it on and stepped into his boots. "I'll call you in the morning?"

"Yeah, that would be great."

Rhys opened the door. Giant snowflakes drifted in like balls of cotton from the granite-colored sky. Everything within her wanted to pull him back into the warmth… of the cabin, her arms, her life.

"I'll get going then." He stepped out onto the porch. "Lock the door, okay?"

"Oh, don't worry, I will. Be safe." She caught herself before reaching out her hand and following the instincts of her aching heart. Having him here had ushered in a whole host of memories and emotions. She had a lot to consider, but they both needed space. "Bye."

With doors locked and all outside lights kept on, she switched off the fire and music before trudging upstairs with her phone. A call to Alexis was on her to-do list as soon as she'd soaked the day's stress from her body in lavender-infused hot water.

In a matter of minutes, she luxuriated in a bubble bath fit for a queen. A lit candle flickered on the marble countertop as she rested her head against the back of the tub and breathed in the soothing fragrance now permeating the room.

Yet her brain swirled with thoughts of Rhys. His reaction was as she had feared. Of course, he would be upset but added into that were his issues with alcohol. She prayed this news wouldn't set him back in any way.

Lord, You know him better than I do. Would You comfort him and let him know he's forgiven? That I want to be… friends?

She cringed as she remembered God knew her heart and her thoughts better than she knew herself. How could she hide the flutter in her belly at the thought of those strong arms encircling her in a tender hug? The way he raked his long fingers through his hair and made her want to feel the thickness of it. His kissable lips sipping hot chocolate. The raw attraction between them was undeniable—and rekindled her hope of a possible reconnection.

A strange scraping sound stilled her musings. The noise came from downstairs. Outside maybe? She sat upright, clutching her knees under her chin, and sending a slosh of water to the rim of the tub. She forced a breath through her lips and froze in place, every nerve in her body on high alert.

Seconds stretched. Silence filled the cabin. Nothing. Should have kept the Christmas music playing downstairs. She was freaking herself out. The noise could be anything if it was outside—there was no shortage of wildlife up here at the lake. Raccoons, deer, an occasional cougar even. And always, the threat of a bear—her worst-case scenario. Perhaps with more homes up here now, she was safer. Wasn't she?

Just as she talked herself into sinking back beneath the bubbles, the scraping sounded again. A scratching. Something being moved. Definitely at the back of the house.

Carla clambered out of the tub, grabbed a fluffy white towel from the rack, and wrapped it around herself. She slid on her glasses and checked her phone. *Please let there be service.* Reception could be spotty sometimes. Yes, she had bars. Although, how long would the police take to get here if she actually needed help? Why didn't she insist Alexis stay here tonight with

Lily? So much for getting her brave on and moving forward.

Leaving a trail of water behind her, she tiptoed along the hallway and stood at the top of the stairs, her long, wet hair dripping down her back. *God, help me.* The noise had stopped, but she needed to check out the back door or she would have no chance of sleeping tonight. She snagged her coat on the way past the rack and bundled it over her towel-clad body. Next, she selected a poker from beside the fireplace. *Just in case.* The glow from the kitchen appliances lit her path to the back door.

A deep breath. No way she was going to open that door—a horrible sense of deja vu filled her with dread. She simply needed to see if anything—or anyone—was on the back porch. With trembling fingers, she tugged the blind that covered the windowpane in the door and peered into the winter evening. Breathe. No one was out there. She looked along the width of the window so she could see most of the porch lit by the twinkly lights. The Christmas tree was still in place, and nothing appeared to have been tampered with.

She leaned her ear against the door and waited several beats. Silence. Had she imagined the earlier noise? The scraping could have been a raccoon, after all. Perhaps if she saw tiny prints out there in the fresh snow, her mind would be put at ease. She might even get some sleep. She checked her phone. Not even nine o'clock? Exhaustion hit after a long day traveling. Okay, she would check out the prints and then head to bed with a book—and leave soft music playing so she didn't wig out again.

A band-aid rip was in order. She set her phone on a side table, held the poker at the ready, and in one smooth move, unlocked the door and swung it open. For a second, she realized how ridiculous she looked in her towel-coat combo, soaking hair, and a fire poker held like a sword. *If Rhys could see me now…* As she scanned the vicinity as far as the lights allowed, nothing seemed amiss at first glance. She let out the breath she'd been holding and dropped her gaze to the ground, where a thin layer of snow had blown under the porch overhang, and there in the middle...

No.

She jumped back inside, slammed the door shut, and locked it. Her heart pounded so hard in her chest, it hurt.

She clutched the poker with both hands as tears filled her eyes.

No racoon could have left those man-sized boot prints.

Chapter Six

RHYS GRIPPED THE STEERING WHEEL AND clenched his jaw as he took the winding roads back down to his vacation rental in town.

Oh, Carla. His vision blurred, and he blinked back tears as he replayed the conversation with her. He'd imagined confessing his addiction to alcohol and how he'd lied to her would be humbling and shameful. Left her with no explanation, just that pathetic note. But to now know that she'd been *attacked* as a result of being alone after he'd acted so selfishly? *Oh Lord, I'm so sorry.*

The chocolate orange fudge from earlier sat like a boulder in his churning stomach as he imagined Carla's desperate screams for help that day. He'd failed her. Hadn't been there for her. Now, his dark thoughts began to spiral around and around like the final dregs of dirty water circling a sink. If only he could make his thoughts stop, bury them in booze like he used to. No alcohol had passed his lips in four years, three months, and twenty-one days. Still, when he was alone with his thoughts like now, and he was far from the nearest AA meeting, his resolve would threaten to crumble.

He checked his rearview mirror, and seeing he had the road to himself, he pulled over, keeping his hazards blinking. Just a few minutes to calm his screeching nerves. He blew out a long, steady breath that mingled with the hot stream of air blasting from the car's vent.

Burying his face in his hands, he did the only thing he knew would really work.

"God, help me. Help Carla. You know my weaknesses, and I know You are my only hope of strength. This news was… a lot. I don't know what to do with it other than to give it to You." He swallowed. "And Carla? Well, I hate what she went through that Christmas Eve, but I thank You for being her Rock. For giving her that heart of kindness and grace that I once fell in love with." Who was he fooling? Nothing had changed, though he'd been in denial.

He still loved her.

His phone rang, and he went to silence it and get back to his prayer. Carla's name appeared on the screen. His fingers squeezed around the phone. Why would she be calling so soon after sending him home?

"Carla, are you okay?"

Silence filled the airwaves for several beats, and then her shaky voice came across in a whisper. "Rhys, did you by any chance go out on my back porch this evening?"

What? "No. No, I only came in through the front door. Why?"

"It could be nothing, but there are footprints." A shuddering breath. "Footprints outside my back door. Man-sized. There's probably some explanation—"

He checked the rearview mirror, dropped his foot on the gas pedal, and made a U-turn. "I'm spinning around now. I'll be there as soon as I can."

"Rhys, I don't—"

He balanced the phone between his shoulder and ear. "I'm on my way. I'll sleep outside in my car if I have to."

"You'll freeze to death."

"I'll check the cabin. Grab some blankets from you. I'm not leaving you alone up there again. It'll be fine. You'll be fine, I promise."

"Morning." Carla yawned as she stumbled into the kitchen and smiled at her sister, who was perched on a stool at the island. "I see Lily made herself at home by the fire." She grabbed an elastic from her wrist and piled her hair into a messy bun. "I can't believe it's past nine already. Been here long?"

Alexis looked up from her laptop and stretched her arms above her head. "An hour or so. I didn't want to wake you, so I got on with some work. Lily decided the love seat was a great place for a nap. Talking of sleep, did you get much after all that excitement?" She closed her laptop and picked up a mug. "Rhys left, by the way." She nodded at a bundle of fleece blankets piled in the corner. "He took off after I arrived. Left the blankets on the porch."

"Really?" Carla's heart sank. So, he didn't want to stick around and talk. Or even have breakfast. "Yeah, I guess I slept well eventually. It helped having Rhys keeping watch out there."

"I'll bet it did." An edge clipped Alexis's voice.

The enticing aroma of rich coffee filled the room, and Carla made a beeline for the espresso machine. She squeezed her sister's arm on her way past. "You should be grateful he doubled back so I didn't have to drag you up here last night." She grabbed a mug from the shelf. "I thought I'd be okay."

"I'm glad you at least phoned me. I was pretty anxious to get up here this morning." She drained her drink. "The footprint mystery is weird, I'm not going to lie. The prints just disappeared without leaving a trail?"

"Rhys checked them out when he came back last night. Said other than on the back porch, he couldn't tell where they went. It was snowing heavy by then."

Alexis huffed as she padded over to the fridge and pulled out a bag of bagels. "Perhaps he didn't look hard enough." She took a knife from the drawer, sliced the bagels, and stuffed them into the toaster.

Carla watched in silence as she continued working on her cappuccino, grateful that her college job at a coffee shop had actually come in useful in real life.

"Listen, if I get a chance, I'll ask around and see if anyone else up here has had any trouble lately." Alexis knew everyone. Shouldn't be a problem.

"That would be great. Thanks."

"Watch the bagels, will you? I'm going to make sure everything's ready for your special guest before I get going for a house showing in town. I'm guessing my services won't be required tonight?" With one hand on her hip, she was the bossy big sister all over again.

"I can take care of everything. You're more than welcome to stay over with Madison and me tonight. It could be fun."

"Thanks, but I don't think so." Alexis stomped up the stairs, and Carla's cell phone rang in her pajama pocket. She pulled it out. Rhys.

"Carla, hey. How are you feeling this morning?" She heard sizzling in the background. Bacon? Perhaps he was making his own breakfast. "Is Alexis still there with you?"

"I'm good, and she's here." She bit her lower lip. "Thanks for sticking around last night. I'm sure you didn't get much sleep in the car." She left her coffee on the counter, walked through the living room, and opened the curtains at the front window. He'd stayed out there all night. She blinked at the bright sky and marvelled at the view of the lake beyond the drive. "Did you at least get to see the sun rise over the lake?"

"I did. Always my favorite time of day. Plus it wasn't too bad in the car. I was warm enough. I'm still concerned about those footprints out back though. I've been thinking, could it have been anyone else? Neighbor checking in on you?"

Her shoulders relaxed. That was a possibility, wasn't it? "Maybe. Alexis is going to ask around. I don't really know anyone up here that well anymore." She moved to the back window and swished open the curtains there. Everything looked serene in the morning sunshine.

He grunted. "Pretty weird to come around back of the cabin though. You'd think someone would knock at the front door."

"True." She chewed on her thumbnail and wandered into the kitchen. "I don't know what to think."

"Do you want me to drive up later? I feel like we should talk again after last night's conversation."

She leaned against the counter and stared at the box of his fudge on the island. "You don't have to, Rhys."

"I want to. If you're comfortable, that is."

How awkward was this conversation? She took a fortifying sip of her coffee. The warmth spread through her body. Maybe a face-to-face would be easier. "Hmm. Madison is flying in soon. I'd planned on bringing her into town maybe late afternoon when it's all pretty and lit up. Grab some dinner."

"Save you from cooking?"

She grinned. "My repertoire hasn't grown much in the past five years, I'm afraid." The bagels popped up from the toaster, and she put the phone on speaker while she looked for cream cheese in the fridge. "You could come up to the cabin this evening. As long as you're comfortable being outnumbered. Madison's husband, Luke, doesn't arrive until Christmas Eve."

"It would be nice to meet her before the party in Seattle. Sure. Ah, will Alexis be there?"

Carla chuckled. "You scared of her?" She gathered two plates and a knife and slathered the bagels with cream cheese.

"Not scared, but after I caused you all that heartache, I can't imagine I'm on her list of favorite people. I think she almost growled at me when she saw me outside in the car this morning."

Carla attempted to keep a straight face and picked up the phone. "Don't worry, she's heading to work soon. She knows I'll be safe with Madison here. She doesn't want me up here alone, that's all."

"Understandable. Would you like me to bring some dessert for you ladies? As Madison booked me to cater her event, it could be like a legit sample."

"Seriously?" This was sounding better by the second.

"Sure. Text me when you're on your way back up to the cabin."

She twirled a strand of hair in her fingers. The huskiness in his voice brought back the familiar, the things she had loved and missed. How could she refuse? "That would be wonderful."

"Enjoy your day and call if you need me."

"I will. Thanks, Rhys." She set the phone on the counter and stared at it.

What was happening? She had prayed for clarity. For a way to work through what had happened, to forgive Rhys and her attacker and be able to move on. To start dreaming of a real relationship and a future that included a family and a home. Would that include Rhys? This was getting complicated.

"Was that his highness?" Alexis hurried into the kitchen, smoothing her black satin blouse into the waistband of her jeans.

"It was." Carla pushed a plate across the island toward Alexis and kept one in front of her. "I'm guessing one of these was for me?"

"Sure. So, what did he say?"

Carla took a deep breath and explained that he was coming to the cabin that evening. "Also, he's bringing dessert as he wants to meet Madison." She picked up her mug and took a sip. She needed the caffeine.

"Are you two starting something again? After the way he treated you?" Alexis spoke around the bagel. "Sis, you really need to learn to protect your heart."

Carla nearly choked on her coffee. "Excuse me? I'm the one who's been in full-on protect-my-heart mode for the past five years. I've been too nervous around men to even think of a real relationship. I've buried myself in my work—which I love—but I'm finally starting to feel ready to be brave. I'm sorry that the only guy I feel safe around is the one who broke my heart, but he knows me. And now he knows the whole truth. So maybe there's a chance he still wants to be in my life." She nibbled on her bagel.

Alexis wiped her mouth with a paper napkin. "Whatever. You're a grown woman."

"He's making dessert for my boss and me. He's not bringing a diamond engagement ring with him." Carla's cheeks were on fire. The last thing she wanted to do was fight with her sister, especially at Christmas. "Hey, why don't you come, too? Meet us for dinner and drive back up here for the night. It'll be great." She rounded the island and hugged Alexis's stiff frame.

"Do you really think I could keep my thoughts to myself with that guy, even if he comes bearing dessert? Besides, I have a bunch of work to do, but I *will* meet you and Madison for dinner downtown. A girl's gotta eat."

"I'd like that." Carla gave Alexis one last squeeze. "I should get showered and ready before she arrives. Do you want me to watch Lily for you?"

Alexis looked over at the love seat where the snoring bulldog had now found a particularly comfortable fur throw to sleep on. "You can if you like. She's a pathetic guard dog and will lick an intruder to death, but she does sound quite ferocious if you can get her to bark. In fact, you're welcome to keep her overnight if you want. It'll save me driving up here to collect her, and she really is good company. There's plenty of dog food in the pantry. I keep a stock of it up here in case it's needed."

"Perfect. A sleepover it is." Carla paused to give Lily's ears a rub on her way toward the stairs. "I'll make sure she gets some fresh air before we head out."

"As long as she has food and a comfy couch, she's set." Alexis squatted down next to her dog and gave her some attention. "I'll leave in a minute. I'll have my phone on all day so call if you need me."

Carla turned at the bottom of the staircase. "I will. Thanks again. I mean, for being here for me."

"Always. Someone has to be."

She had a point, but her words still grated. "I'll try to keep the excitement to a minimum for the rest of my stay."

"Why, thank you." Alexis raised a brow. "That would be nice."

An hour later, the sound of tires crackled on the packed snow outside the cabin, and Carla rushed to the front door and swung it wide open. "Hey, I'll be right out there to give you a hand." She stuffed her feet in the snow boots she'd found in her closet.

"No need." Madison grinned as she walked around the rental car. "I only have one rolling case. Stay in the warm."

"If you insist." Carla held the door open and soon enveloped her friend in a hug. "I'm so glad you're here. Come on in. You look great."

Madison didn't look as if she'd been traveling overnight; her chocolate-brown eyes sparkled, and long, dark ringlets tumbled over her shoulders. Then again, she never looked anything but perfectly put together, even in the humidity of Mexico amidst an orphanage full of rambunctious children.

"Thanks—I'm not going to lie; I feel like flying alone is the height of indulgence for me these days. A good book, a nap, peace and quiet."

Carla had felt the same on her own flight yesterday. "You're missing the kids already."

"Absolutely. You, too?"

"So much." She took Madison's faux fur jacket and rolled her case against the wall. "I'm impressed you wanted to drive up here. You didn't mind the snow?"

"No. They seem to keep the roads in decent shape. I thought it would add to the adventure." She took in the cabin's interior. "This is so magical. Wow. I thought you said it was rustic." She chuckled. "Clearly, my idea of rustic and yours are miles apart."

"Oh, trust me. This place had a major upgrade since I was here last. I don't hate it one bit. Come and take a look around. I'll get some coffee going. Unless you'd prefer tea?"

Madison left her leather boots by the door and followed. "I think caffeine is a good idea if I'm going to get through the rest of the day. Thanks." She spotted Lily on the couch. "Who do we have here?" She bent over the bulldog, who hadn't stopped snoring, and tickled her ears.

"Lily belongs to my sister. I'm borrowing her for the day. Kind of a sleepy guard dog."

"So cute." Madison followed Carla into the kitchen. "Seriously, this place is gorgeous. I had no idea the lake was right at the front of the property. I can see why you wanted to come back." She looked through the rear window at the mountainous backdrop and exhaled. "It's so… Canadian."

Carla smiled. "Really?"

"Sorry, I'll try not to be too tourist-y, but you know how much I've been looking forward to seeing where you grew up. *Hollybrook*. It sounds like something from a Christmas movie."

"It has its cute features, I guess. Not all memories are sweet though." She wrapped her arms around her middle.

Madison tilted her head to one side. "Did you speak with your ex?"

"Yeah." Her voice cracked, and her chin trembled.

"Wanna talk about it, lovely?" Madison walked over and put an arm around Carla's shoulder, her eyes full of compassion. She'd experienced loss, betrayal, and even kidnapping in her own life and was tender toward Carla whenever they spoke of Rhys. Now seemed like the right time to share *all* of the story about that Christmas Eve five years ago. And maybe pick Madison's brain for some wisdom in how to move forward without getting her heart broken all over again.

Although, she had a horrible feeling she might be too late.

Chapter Seven

"SO, THIS IS THE HEART OF the downtown area." Carla pulled her toque down over her chilly ears and linked an arm through Madison's as they strolled down Main Street. Twinkling lights were strung on every tree and storefront, and a loudspeaker outside the city hall played Christmas carols on repeat. Yes, she'd missed the cozy charm that oozed from Hollybrook's hub in the festive season.

"I love it." Madison clapped her mittens together. "Is that the library across the street?" She lowered her voice. "Where you and Rhys met?"

"Yes." Carla's stomach flipped as she recalled the heart stopping moment she first laid eyes on him. "That's where we literally bumped into each other, and my stack of books toppled all over the sidewalk." A lifetime ago. Was she crazy to think they may have a chance to rekindle a relationship? She blinked and pointed across the road. "*This* is where we're meeting Alexis for dinner." The cozy Italian restaurant was bookended by a post office and a bakery. "I hope it's still as good as it used to be." She checked her phone for messages. "Oh, Alexis texted already. She's inside. Let's get out of the cold."

"I'm not going to argue with that."

On the other side of the street, Carla opened the restaurant door and followed Madison inside, where they both stomped their snowy boots on the large mat in the foyer. The sudden warmth was a welcome relief, and within seconds, Carla was able to feel her cheeks again. "That's better. You doing okay?"

She turned to Madison, who had tucked her chin beneath a cream wool scarf but couldn't hide her red nose.

"I will be. I'm just thankful you had warmer clothes for me to borrow. I'm not used to these temperatures."

"After five years in Mexico, neither am I." Carla surveyed the restaurant and spotted Alexis on her phone seated in the back corner. She smiled at the pretty teenaged host and pointed at the table. "My sister's over there in the back."

"Perfect. Come with me." The host grabbed several menus and led the way, followed by Madison and then Carla. When they reached the table, the host set down the menus, and Alexis looked up with a tentative smile.

"It's so lovely to finally meet you." Madison grinned and took the chair opposite Alexis. She gushed about Hollybrook and how lucky Alexis was to live in such a beautiful place.

Carla slid into the chair next to Madison, and smirked when Alexis's somewhat frosty exterior softened into slush after talking with Madison for only a few minutes. This woman was a miracle-worker. Perhaps she could also put in a good word about Rhys.

While they chatted, Carla watched the other patrons enjoying steaming plates of pasta and the famous in-house pizzas. The aroma of cheese wafted in the air mixed with garlic and spices—she would have to indulge in a feta cheese and beef pizza, if it was still on the menu. How many times had she and Rhys enjoyed that particular favorite with a glass of wine? She bit her lip. How had she not seen his struggle with alcohol?

A couple entered the restaurant and caught her eye. Carla cocked her head. Why did the woman look familiar?

"Do you know what you'll have?" Madison passed a huge menu to Carla. "Everything sounds divine."

"I can recommend the pizza." She touched her sister's hand. "Hey, do I know that couple who just came in? They're sitting at the table in the front window, but don't stare."

Alexis swiveled in her chair and stared. "Yes. They work for me. Remember I almost ran over Sarah-Jane yesterday?"

"Oh dear." Madison's eyes widened. "That sounds awful."

"It's all good." Alexis shrugged and turned back to their conversation. "She's a bit ditsy and is in a world of her own most of the time. She cleans the cabin. He's a handyman, bit of a jack-of-all trades."

Carla tried to look over as subtly as possible, but she caught the man's eye. His piercing stare caused a ripple to run right through her. She averted her eyes and recognized the blonde couple at the next table. "Hey, Alexis, is that Thomas and Tessa in the corner?"

"Sure is." She leaned across to Madison. "They literally started dating when they were in sixth grade and were doomed to get married from the start."

"Doomed?" Carla wrinkled her nose.

"Destined. Whatever. Anyway, they're both residents at the hospital. They're actually a really cool couple. I got them their current townhouse, and I'm hoping they'll remember me when they want their mansion one day." Alexis down set her menu. "I'm having lasagna."

Carla grinned. *I've missed my cynical big sister.* "Want to share a pizza, Madison?"

"Don't forget to save room for Rhys's dessert." Alexis checked her perfect nails. "If that's still on the agenda. Tell me, Madison, what are your thoughts on the man who broke my little sister's heart?"

Carla closed her eyes and said a prayer as Madison attempted to douse Alexis's cutting remarks with kindness.

This was going to be a long dinner.

Back at the cabin, Carla's full stomach churned in anticipation. Rhys would be here any minute, and she still had no clue how she was supposed to feel about him.

"You okay?" Madison stifled a yawn behind her hand as she snuggled up against a sleeping Lily, who had only moved briefly for food and a bathroom break. "You seem awfully jittery. I'm pretty sure you've changed up the Christmas music three times, and you've karate chopped that pillow twice already. Relax."

"Ugh." Carla flopped onto the love seat. "I'm confused. Is this really a good idea? Having Rhys here tonight, I mean. I knew I needed to speak with him to verbally forgive him for the way he ended our relationship, and to tell him everything else that happened. I can check that off my list. Plus, I've made peace with this cabin."

"Even knowing someone was on the back porch last night?" Madison winced. "Sorry to bring that up."

"There has to be a reason for those footprints. Or maybe they weren't as fresh as I suspected." Although, her own footprints from earlier had been covered by evening. "Anyway, I'm focusing on all the great memories I have here. So many. I think even my relationship with Alexis is in a good place—as good as it's ever been really. We're very different people, and sometimes, it's hard to meet in the middle."

"She's looking out for you, that's all. Maybe being here with you right after that awful attack had more of an effect on her than you realize." Madison pulled her feet up and tugged a fur throw over her lap. "She seems a strong woman, but it's clear she's protective of her little sister. Especially with your parents being so far away."

"True. What am I going to do about Rhys?" Carla stared up at the beamed ceiling and inhaled a waft of peppermint from the candle flickering on the coffee table.

Madison twirled a long strand of hair between her fingers. "Do you still have strong feelings for him? After all this time?"

Heat flooded Carla's face and not from the warmth of the fireplace. "Honestly, yes. It's so unexpected. I thought I might be angry with him face-to-face. Or perhaps I was hoping he was already married or a complete jerk or had shrivelled into some kind of unappealing specimen I wouldn't look at twice."

"But he's as kind as you remember? Before he left that note, I mean."

"Yes, and as handsome. Maybe even more so." Carla hugged a cushion to her chest. "Wait and see. I'd value your opinion. I could be viewing him through rose tinted glasses."

"Or simply through those funky red frames, which happen to look amazing, by the way."

Carla adjusted her newest pair of glasses on her slender nose. "Thanks. I was going for confident with these babies." Rhys had always liked the way she changed up her glasses depending on her mood.

Beams of filtered light shone through the closed curtains at the front of the cabin, and the crunch of packed snow sounded from the driveway. Lily let out a low rumble from her throat without moving from the couch.

"Looks like I won't have to wait long to meet him." Madison discarded the throw, rushed over to Carla, and tugged her to her feet. "Be yourself. You'll do great."

"Right." She straightened her navy sweater and took a deep breath as she padded over to the front door and opened it wide.

"Hi." A light dusting of snow covered Rhys's hair like icing sugar, and Carla's fingers itched to brush away the delicate flakes. She balled her fists.

"Come on in. Meet Madison." Carla unfurled her hands and accepted the covered platter from him. She winked at Madison as she headed to the kitchen, where soothing strains of festive jazz filled the air.

Madison made small talk with Rhys in the foyer before they joined Carla at the kitchen island.

"Tea, coffee, hot chocolate?" Knowing better than to offer wine, Carla held her palms up and waited for someone else to decide.

"Well, what do we have for dessert?" Madison perched on a stool. "That could sway my decision."

Rhys grinned at Carla. "Guess."

"Not sugarplum snowflakes." Her hands flew to her face. "Really?"

He nodded and set a small box on the counter next to his platter. "I thought I should allow Madison to sample the dessert she chose for her upcoming party. It's the least I could do. Molly let me use the kitchen at Angel Cakes bakery to whip up a batch." He nodded at the box. "I also brought Earl Grey tea bags, just in case."

"Perfect." Madison jumped up. "Where can I find little plates?"

Carla pointed to the upper cupboards. "Try one of those. I'll grab mugs." She opened the box of tea and fished out three bags.

Madison located plates as well as forks. "You won't hear me complaining about dessert samples. My sister, Chloe, raved about your business so much. You've made quite the impression on the Seattle food scene."

"Thanks. That's kind of her to say so." He peeled the wrap from his platter, and Carla caught a glimpse of the stunning snowflake desserts before turning back to the kettle.

While the others chatted about food and Seattle, all Carla could think of as she poured the hot water over the tea bags was the last time she'd eaten this special sweet. He'd been experimenting for weeks with different variations of festive goodies, until she had suggested creating a snowflake version.

After all, snowflakes had been their thing. Their emblem, really. First, they'd made those silly popsicle-stick snowflakes for the sparse little Christmas tree. Then, he found a pair of silver snowflake earrings for her at a local market. She had bought him a glass snowflake paperweight for Christmas—that she didn't give to him because he left.

"Carla?" She spun around at the sound of Rhys's voice. "What do you think?" He held out a plate of dessert, looking like a little boy seeking parental approval for a science project.

She carried the teas to the island and smiled at the scrumptious work of art before her. "Wow." A deep purple "plum" sat amidst a bed of white chocolate shavings, coated in sparkling sugar, and topped with an intricate white chocolate snowflake. "It's beautiful. You've made some improvements, I see." She rotated the plate and inspected the offering. "Glad you kept the white chocolate. Good decision."

His brow furrowed. Was he also remembering the last time they ate this dessert together? Days before he ran away.

"Oh. My. Goodness." Madison's eyes bugged. "It tastes even better than it looks." She shook her head. "You have to tell me what is in this plum because it's not a plum. That much I know."

Rhys touched Carla's shoulder briefly—perhaps reassurance that this brought back memories for him, too?

He turned his attention to Madison. "Yeah, it's crazy, but there are no actual plums in sugarplums. I've added my own caramel twist to the usual spices, honey, dried fruits, and a long list of random ingredients." He stuffed both hands in his pockets. "You can thank Carla for the white chocolate snowflake idea."

"Really?" Madison raised her fork. "You know my affection for chocolate. Nice work, friend."

"Thanks."

A joyful tune rang out from Madison's phone that sat on the counter. "Oh, I should get this, it's Luke. Will you excuse me? I'll take this yumminess with me."

"Of course. Say hi to him and send my love to the kids." Carla shooed her upstairs and perched on a stool. She bit into her snowflake. The treat was pure creamy indulgence and by far the best white chocolate she'd ever tasted. "You've taken everything up a notch, Rhys."

"It's been years in the perfecting." He took a swig of tea and sat next to her.

Like you? Carla couldn't help wonder if the dessert was the only thing that had been years in the perfecting. *Has God chiseled away at you like He has with me?* She longed to ask the hard, deep questions. She took another bite and chewed.

"Are you good? With this, I mean?" His voice was soft as he gestured toward the platter of sugarplums. "Does it feel awkward?"

She shook her head, and her long hair fell across her shoulders. "Not awkward at all, actually." Could he see her hands trembling as she clutched the fork? She set it down on her plate.

Their eyes locked, and seconds stretched out while a saxophone rendition of "In the Bleak Midwinter" played in the air that crackled between them.

"Glad you came home for a snow-on-snow Christmas?" He broke the hush. Oh, how she'd missed the gentle timbre of his voice. And this cabin—this sense of… belonging. Nostalgia was messing with her head.

"I am." How was she supposed to eat when he was watching her every move? She wanted to say so much.

A torrent of questions she'd wanted to ask. Now, her mouth couldn't form more than two words. "You?"

Another swig of tea. "This may not officially be home for me, but it feels like a very special place. I've had trouble settling down anywhere, if I'm going to be honest. Seattle's where I was born and raised, and I'd hoped it would feel like home after my stint in France."

"But it doesn't?"

He wrinkled his nose. "I'm trying, but it feels like I'm forcing it. Trying extra hard to feel comfortable, which is…"

"Uncomfortable?" She'd been feeling that way in Mexico of late. Like wearing an ill-fitting pair of shoes, she was going through the motions, yet life didn't seem as snug and satisfying as before.

"Exactly, but living here in Hollybrook for that year? That's where I have most of my happy memories stashed. Partly because my uncle brought me here on vacation when I was a kid. And partly because of…"

"Us?" The word came out on a whisper.

He put down his mug and stood in front of her. "I'm sorry." He went to touch her face, then stuffed both of his hands in his pockets. "I'll never stop being sorry."

She froze on the stool, not wanting to shatter the moment.

He drew in a deep breath. "For what I did to you and for what happened afterwards."

She slid down and placed the palms of her hands on his chest. "I'm sorry it happened, too."

With a slight moan, he wrapped his arms around her and spoke into her hair. "I've made some mistakes…" He squeezed tighter.

Feeling the weight of his arms around her was like the warmest blanket. Oh, how she missed being held like this. Like she mattered. "I can feel your sincerity." She rested her cheek against his beating heart and breathed in his cologne that reminded her of the ocean. "God will help us heal; I know He will. We both have to move on from all of that." She willed herself to believe those words, cradled in the safety of his arms.

"You're right." He pulled back, a sheen of moisture covering his hazel eyes as he held both her hands. "You'll never know how grateful I am that you had the courage and the kindness to reach out. To give me a chance to ask for forgiveness."

"Trust me, it's only because I have God giving me the strength. And the grace." She gave his hands a squeeze.

"I get it. He's been my rock, too. If it hadn't been for Him, I would never have met—"

"I'm so sorry about that." Madison's voice grew louder, and Carla stepped back from Rhys's nearness. Madison rushed into the kitchen, a smile dancing across her face. "I had to tell Luke all about this place. He's going to absolutely love it."

Carla glanced at Rhys, wondering what he was about to share. "Yeah, I'm sure he will. Hey, why don't we go and sit by the fire? Lily looks lonely over there."

"Sounds good." Madison dumped her empty plate in the sink.

Carla forked the last piece of her sugarplum snowflake into her mouth, savoring the richness before she swallowed. "Anyone want more dessert? Rhys, you didn't eat any at all."

He grinned. "A little too much taste testing this afternoon. But please, put the rest in the fridge for you guys tomorrow."

"Thanks." Carla found a container and transferred the remaining sweets. "I won't argue with that."

"I'm absolutely stuffed." Madison carried her tea into the living room and sank down on a love seat. "I must say it really was exquisite."

"I still can't believe how chic this place is now." Rhys admired the perfect Christmas tree as he followed and sat on the love seat opposite Madison, crossing one leg over the other.

"I know." Carla joined Lily on a soft rug on the floor, where she'd found a warm sleeping area by the fireplace. "It'll fetch a pretty penny."

Rhys tilted his head. "Come again?"

Carla let out a groan. "Alexis is putting it up for sale."

"Really? I'm surprised she's selling it after all these years." He ran a hand down his face. "Your parents don't want it anymore?"

"Apparently not. It's a sensible option for them financially for their future. They're missionaries, after all."

"Missionary life can be unpredictable." Madison sipped her tea. "Luke has told me so many stories of his years not knowing where his next paycheck would come from. It's not for the faint of heart."

"He's a missionary, too?" Rhys's eyes lit up. "Cool."

"She snagged him at her sister's wedding in Jamaica." Carla winked. "The single missionary was smitten. Nicely done."

Madison laughed. "It's a long story, but it was all meant to be. Now I get to share his life and his love for a bunch of beautiful children in Mexico."

"That's amazing." Rhys looked over at Carla. "Then you got to meet this special lady."

Carla caught his eye and felt her cheeks burn.

Madison chuckled. "I did indeed. We became friends right away. I don't know what we'd all do without her."

Carla's insides churned. She hadn't even hinted at her thoughts about leaving Mexico yet. The move would be tough if she decided to follow through.

God, You're going to have to make it crystal clear to me if and when it's time to start a new chapter.

Madison drained her tea and stood. "I hate to be a party-pooper, but the travel has caught up with me. I think I'll have to call it a night."

Rhys stood. "It was really nice to meet you in person."

"Likewise." She gave him a quick side hug. "Will we be seeing you again before the party in Seattle?"

Carla held her breath. She felt a crazy urge to spend as much time with this man as possible. *I need to keep my heart in check here.*

"Maybe." He resumed his position on the love seat. "My flight back to Seattle is on Christmas Eve, but I'm free all day tomorrow."

"Great." Madison leaned down and hugged Carla. "I may sleep in for a while to catch up from last night's lack of sleep, so go ahead and… do what you have to do." She gave a wink.

"Sure. Thanks. Sleep well. I'll try not to wake you in the morning." Carla rubbed Lily's head. "Right, pup?"

Madison made her way upstairs and for several moments, only Christmas music filled the cozy cabin.

"So, how's everything going in Mexico?" Rhys's voice was low. "Are you on a contract or settled there indefinitely?" He smoothed his hands down his pant legs.

A not-so-subtle question. Carla lifted a shoulder. "No contract." She matched his whisper. "To be honest, I'm feeling restless. I adore my job, and the kids are delightful, yet… I don't know, I've got itchy feet. I think I miss home." She looked up at him. "I miss this place. I guess I secretly dreamed I'd come back one day."

"I get it."

She lifted a brow. "Why do you ask? Curious about my dreams?"

He leaned forward on the love seat. "Actually, there is something we need to talk about." His voice was normal volume now, and that crease between his brows was extra pronounced, a sign that he was serious.

Carla swallowed. What could possibly be more serious than what they'd already discussed? The hairs on the back of her neck prickled, and she left Lily on the floor so she could be eye-to-eye with him on the opposite love seat. "Go ahead." She squeezed the sofa's soft leather arm and braced for what might come next. "I feel like we've been more honest with each other in the past twenty-four hours than we were in our entire relationship before."

He balked.

"Sorry. I didn't mean for it to come out like that." She bit on a thumbnail.

"No, it's true. A hundred percent. I lived a lie for a really long time, and I'm not proud of it."

"That's in the past." *Right, Lord?*

He gripped his knees. "In the spirit of being honest and open, I need to tell you about someone."

Ugh. His sordid past. He was bound to have skeletons in his closet from the time before he got his life together.

She raised her chin. "Please do."

"Okay. It's Gabriella." His ears burned red to the tips.

Pretty name. "Who was Gabriella?"

"It's complicated." A muscle popped in his jaw, and he looked down at his hands. "But she's my fiancée."

Chapter Eight

Carla closed her mouth and hugged her knees to her chest. "Your fiancée?"

How foolish had she been to not even ask if Rhys was in a serious relationship? Just because his website didn't mention a wife, that didn't mean he wasn't married. Or *engaged.*

He made eye contact with her and swallowed. "I know I should have mentioned her before."

That would have been nice. "Congratulations." She choked the word out and even attempted a wobbly smile. She had wanted to be his fiancée once upon a time. She'd been so sure an engagement would happen between them. That Christmas five years ago, she suspected a proposal might even occur—only to be dumped and left in the dust. *What is the matter with me?*

After an awkward silent pause, a jazz rendition of "O Holy Night" began playing, and Carla had no clue what to say next. She wanted to know when he was getting married, if this woman was anything like her, how he proposed—yet she couldn't stomach another moment. Why put herself through the agony of knowing the details of how he'd moved on?

"You know, I think I'll call it a night, too." She stood and hurried to the kitchen to gather his empty platter. "Thanks for the dessert. Madison was suitably impressed."

He followed and touched her arm. "Hey." He spun her around to face him.

"What?" Tears pooled in her eyes. She would not cry. Not in front of him. No way.

"I should have explained as soon as we started texting. I thought it would be easier face-to-face. Then, it wasn't easy because…"

"Please leave, Rhys." Her voice cracked, and she shoved the platter into his hands and took a step back.

His eyes narrowed, and she recognized pain. The old adage, *you can't have your cake and eat it, too,* fit the moment.

"You don't understand…" His words came out as a whisper.

"I understand completely. You shouldn't be here. Goodbye, Rhys."

He closed his eyes for a moment. "Then I'll see myself out." He squeezed her hand one last time.

She pinched her lips together to stave the blubbering sobs that were about to erupt any second and stood rigid as she watched him leave.

As soon as the front door closed, she locked it, retreated to the living room, and collapsed on the rug by the fire. Her tears soaked into the dog's coarse fur. After several minutes and some meaningful licks on Carla's hands, Lily looked up and let out a soft moan.

"Come on, girl." Carla wiped her face with the cuff of her sweater. "You haven't been outside for hours. I'll let you out before I go to bed. I have a lot of thinking and praying to do."

She shut off the strains of "Auld Lang Syne" and called Lily to the back door.

"Out you go. Don't be long though, it's freezing out there." She opened the door to the lit porch area and looked around to make sure the yard was safe for the dog. No wildlife seemed to be evident, and Lily lumbered through the doorway and onto the porch.

"Hurry." Carla folded her arms across her chest and watched as Lily descended the steps. She looked down and surveyed the length of the porch.

Her stomach clenched.

Boot prints covered the area, intermingled with Lily's. She followed the trail of them with her eyes as they led up to the back door, along to the back window, and then around to the steps. Her entire body trembled. *God, what is going on?*

Her heart beat faster as she called out for Madison and watched Lily disappear behind a tree.

"Madison." She turned back into the cabin and yelled again, hoping her friend wasn't already asleep.

"Coming." Footsteps reverberated as Madison ran down the stairs and joined Carla in the doorway. "What's wrong?" She clutched Carla's hand.

Carla pointed at the prints, their tread mocking her, willing her to never forget what happened out there. "They—they must have been made in the past couple of hours." She looked out into the night. "It's been snowing all evening."

"Oh honey, you go inside. I'll wait for Lily. There's no one here now." Madison flashed the light from her phone into the darkness where the dog's form wandered from tree to tree. "Lily would know."

"I'm not leaving you."

"Then we'll wait together." Madison wrapped her arms around her pajama-clad middle.

Carla slipped her arm around Madison's and drew strength from her presence as she shivered in the winter night until they could safely lock out any sign of danger.

And this time, Carla refused to call Rhys.

After a stressful night of not enough sleep and too much thinking, Carla crawled out of bed around 11:00 AM, took a hot shower, and then dressed in her favorite pale blue sweater and thin black ski-pants. She looked through her bedroom window and made the decision: a snowshoeing session would help clear her head. As long as she was safe.

The footprints scenario kept her awake last night. Twice in a row? She was grateful to have Madison in the cabin with her this time, and the dog had kept guard downstairs. Who was doing this, and what did they want? Nothing was stolen. The door wasn't broken down, and the lock hadn't been tampered with. She'd have to check with Alexis and see if any neighbors mentioned anything suspicious going on in the area.

In the light of day, the situation seemed less daunting, and these trails were her stomping ground. The morning sun shone, and the sky was cobalt blue against the white mountaintops. Perfect. She'd missed hiking these familiar mountain trails. First, she'd take a closer look at the footprints in daylight. See if there had been any more and where they might lead.

No sound came from Madison's room, so Carla crept downstairs and switched on the coffee machine while she checked the back porch. Lily bolted to the back door as soon as she heard the latch and went outside while Carla grabbed her boots from the foyer and slipped into them at the back door. She bypassed the prints on the porch and followed the dog down the steps.

Nothing fresh in the way of prints. She hugged herself and plodded behind Lily to the trees, but no definitive trail of man-sized prints was evident. More snow had fallen in the night, and out where there was no protection from the semi-covered porch, any possible prints had disappeared. She squinted into the distance, and a shiver ran through her. Was someone watching her even now?

Lily snorted as she feasted on snow.

"Come on, girl." Carla tapped her leg. "Let's warm up and get you some real food."

They headed inside, locked the door, and Carla poured dry dog food and fresh water into Lily's stainless-steel bowls. As there had been no new footprints, maybe she'd go ahead as planned and spend time on her beloved mountain. After her shot of caffeine.

If only Madison were awake. They could talk about Rhys and his surprise announcement last night. Engaged? She closed her eyes as she drained her cappuccino. Maybe she'd have a fiancé of her own one day. Too bad the only face that filled her imagination was that of Rhys.

She leaned back on the island and stared through the kitchen window at the back of the cabin to the mountains beyond. "God, You're going to have to help me forget about him."

"Forget about who?" Carla pivoted as Madison tiptoed into the kitchen in red plaid pajamas.

"Sorry if I woke you. I tried to keep the noise to a minimum in the shower. Want me to make you a coffee?"

"It's all good, I can make it. Trust me, I never get to sleep in even this long; it's a treat. I slept great, all things considered. How about you? Those footprints were more than a little disturbing last night."

"I was restless. There haven't been any more prints this morning though, I checked already. It's a mystery where they came from."

"No trail?"

Carla bit her thumbnail. "No. I wish there had been. There was more snow earlier, and I guess it covered over anything obvious. In all the drama I didn't tell you last night about Rhys's news. That's what really kept my mind whirring."

Madison picked up a mug from the draining board and spun around. "Oh?"

Carla blinked several times. "He told me about his fiancée. He's engaged to be married."

"Oh, sweetie." She rushed over and held Carla tight. "That's not what I expected."

"Me neither." Carla pulled back and wiped at a stray tear.

Madison tilted her head. "I don't get it. The way he looks at you…"

"Perhaps it's the way he looks at everyone." Carla took off her glasses and rubbed her tired eyes. "Anyway, I was planning on going for a walk to clear my head. Snowshoeing. Want me to wait for you?"

Madison took her mug over to the espresso machine. "You go on. I'm still adjusting from Mexico temperatures and was considering a long, hot soak in that glorious tub. Is that all right with you?"

Carla chuckled. "Enjoy it while you can. It's not often you haven't got a dozen little ones demanding your attention. Please help yourself to whatever you'd like for breakfast. I recommend the lemon and blueberry muffins."

"I will, thanks. Will you be safe on your own?" Madison narrowed her eyes. "Maybe I *should* come along."

"I'm totally fine. This is my childhood playground, remember? I'll go along the shore of the lake and then head up into the forest area. There's a cute little warming shack not even an hour from here. I used to go there all the time to pray." She let out a heavy sigh. "And I need to pray."

Madison waited until the cappuccino finished gurgling and hissing. "I understand. Plus, you're only here for such a short time."

"I'll lock up and leave Lily here with you for company, and you can call Alexis if you need anything. She'll be awake by now, and I'm sure she'll head up soon to check on Lily. You gave her your number at dinner, didn't you?"

Madison nodded. "Yeah. I'll shoot her a text before my bath just to see what time I can expect her."

"Awesome." Carla would be sure to check in with her sister to see if she'd asked around the neighborhood yet. Alexis may have forgotten if she was engrossed in finishing her work before Christmas.

"Please take care and let's talk later? I'm here for you when you're ready."

"Thanks. I'll be back by two, and we can rustle up a late lunch."

Madison took a long sip of her coffee. "Sounds great."

Carla collected her old gear from the closet under the stairs and slid a water bottle into her tiny backpack.

I'll be safe, won't I?

For a moment, the memory of the footprints on her back porch shook her bravado, but she quickly pushed the thoughts aside.

This was her alone time. Her time with God in His fabulous creation, her time to simply be. To think and to listen. She needed to do this.

The snowshoes felt foreign on her feet after not using them for so many years. She slipped out the front door, careful to lock it behind her, and by the time she'd reached the lakeside trail, snowshoeing felt as natural as walking. Muscle memory. A curious thing.

The lake was covered in snow and was most likely solid. She hadn't noticed anyone skating on the frozen water yet, but then again, she hadn't seen many cars on the road that led up here, and no one was hanging around outside in the cold. Alexis seemed sure the homes were mostly occupied. Maybe everyone worked or were out of town for the holidays. *Christmas Eve is tomorrow.* That wasn't helping her heavy heart. Would Christmas Eve ever be a truly joyful day to celebrate?

While she settled into her snowshoeing rhythm, she thought about holiday seasons from her childhood. They were always so much fun. Always up at the cabin. At lunch time, her family would build a bonfire on the property and make smores and drink hot chocolate. Rosy cheeks, burnt marshmallows, blue mittens knitted by Mom. Every year they were involved in the church Christmas Eve service, so they would get dressed up in their Sunday best and head into town for the early evening candlelight service. Carols, a nativity play, the anticipation of celebrating Christ's birth.

She remembered fighting through exhaustion after a dinner of appetizers and baked goodies in order to listen to Daddy read the Christmas story from his black leather Bible. And then they could open one present. Always a book. Her favorite. Finally, she would read late into the night; a full day, full belly, full heart.

Carla's snowshoes crunched on the packed icy ground, and she exhaled a puff of steam into the frosty air. Man, this place was opening the floodgates for nostalgia. Perhaps because this Christmas would be the last one she would ever spend here at the cabin. That still stung. She squinted at the other wooden homes dotted around the lake, wishing she'd worn sunglasses. The snow dazzled, and some windows reflected the glare from the sun so much it made her eyes hurt to even look. Was anyone watching her? Her scalp prickled.

She couldn't think of anyone she used to know that might still live here. A few older couples who were friends of her grandparents, but they would have either passed away or be in retirement homes by now. A couple of the houses looked new. And big. Surely there must be families there. This would be such a pretty place to settle down and raise a family. She followed the trail away from the lake and up toward the wooded area, bracing herself for a steep incline.

A home, happily married, a few children. Maybe a side hustle she could fit in, doing something she loved with books. Those were Carla's lofty dreams. To some, her goals might seem unremarkable—but to her, if she found the right man, and God led them to their perfect place, she would be more than satisfied. If she had learned one thing over the past few years in Mexico, the truth was that the Christian life was never boring.

Her mind crept to thoughts of Rhys and his fiancée. Gabriella. *Don't think about them, but* she couldn't help herself. Did the woman work? Did she want children? Rhys had always said he wanted three. Carla had joked they would settle on five. Then he left her, and she'd ended up with at least ten kids at a time at the orphanage.

She stopped and turned around. *Huh.* She'd walked a decent way up the trail. The buried lake stretched out below her like a giant frozen puddle. With gathering clouds adding to the dramatic vista, the scene was stunning from her vantage point. Maybe she could persuade Madison to come out with her later if she took some photos and showed her the views. The air didn't even seem as cold now. Probably because she'd been pounding out her frustration on the trail. She stuffed her gloves in her jacket pockets and glanced at her phone screen. Almost out of power. She grimaced. How come the phone hadn't charged last night? She must not have plugged in the cord properly. Just a few pics then.

After berating herself for not checking before she left, Carla snapped several photos, slid her phone back into her pocket, and found her rhythm once again. At this rate, she'd be up at the shack by 12:30 PM, no problem.

With only the sound of her metal clamps crunching the snow, the rest of the world was a delightfully muffled silence, almost as if she had her ears stuffed with cotton balls. Both strange and comforting. She continued through the tallest pine trees heavy with snow, energized by the realization hers were the first prints to traverse the trail this morning.

A flash of something caught in her peripheral vision.

She stopped. Turned her head to the right. Nothing. "Who's there?"

A deer, perhaps. Not a bear at this time of year, surely? Should have dug out some bear spray.

Or is someone else up here?

"Hello?" She swiveled around without moving her feet from their forward position in the cumbersome snowshoes.

Perhaps she'd scared off some wildlife, after all. If she remembered correctly, a cross-country ski trail was nearby—could that glimpse have been a skier flying past? They would pick up speed coming downhill. Yes, she would go with that explanation.

Move on, girl.

That's exactly what she needed to do. Keep moving up the trail, keep moving on with her life, whatever that looked like. As her hip flexors strained and her thighs burned, she prayed in time with the cadence of her steps.

God, I trust You. I know Your plans are best and that nothing takes You by surprise. I feel... unsettled. Like I need to move on to the next chapter in my life. But I have no idea what that even looks like. A relationship? You know how I struggle with trusting men in general, Lord. Rhys is the only one I feel comfortable around and... well, that's obviously history now. Where should I settle down? I thought maybe the cabin was calling me home, but Alexis has made it clear that it's going up for sale. Yet I also feel like my time in Mexico has come to an end, even though I love those kids so much, and Madison and Luke are like my family. What else would I even do?

A branch snapped like a firecracker. Carla stopped. That was way too close. Where had the noise come from?

Her mouth went dry as she spun around full circle in her snowshoes. "Hello?"

Maybe doing this alone wasn't such a great idea.

She was in a dense area now. Tree trunks sprouted from the snow as far as she could see in every direction with her current trail making the only way through. Her options were to plough on or go back. She checked her watch. Forty minutes from the cabin so she would soon be at the little shack.

A minute passed. Then two. Silence surrounded her, and snowflakes began falling through the trees, catching on her eyelashes. She had nothing to fear.

She pulled her toque down over her ears and faced the uphill trail.

"I'm moving on."

Chapter Nine

THERE YOU ARE.

As the trees became less clustered and the sky, now heavy with the promise of more snow, opened up ahead, Carla breathed a sigh of relief. The little wooden shack stood before her like an old friend. She grinned as she left the shelter of the trees behind her and entered the clearing, stepping out onto fresh white powder. The humble structure was exactly as she remembered.

Her imaginary fairy tale. She chuckled as she took the last few steps toward the tiny front porch. She and Alexis used to pretend to be lost in the woods, and then they would take shelter here, sometimes bringing lunch along, too. Of course, their father had been with them in the early years, even their grandpa back when he was agile enough to make the trek up the trail. Then as teens, this was their special place where they shared secrets. Until Alexis outgrew the shack—outgrew her little sister—and then the shack was just for Carla. Her prayer place. She'd even brought Rhys up here. *Oh, Lord.* Her heart twisted. *Help me make some new memories here, would You?*

Carla slumped on the front step and stared out at the scenery as she caught her breath. The view from this spot was spectacular. To the right, mountains dressed in necklaces of white reached to the sky, strong and glorious. On her left, she could see down into the valley, where Hollybrook would be bustling with holiday preparations. Somewhere straight ahead, her lake was hidden by a plethora of pines, a slew of real Christmas trees. This. This was what she had missed. The peace. The pure, clean air. Christmas at home.

A shiver ran through her body. She'd worked up a sweat and needed to get inside the shack before she caught a chill.

Unhooking her snowshoes, she leaned them against the porch rail and plodded up the steps, her boots now light as air. Someone had replaced the door handle. She was foolish to imagine nobody had been here since her last visit, yet the notion of other people encroaching upon her memories stung a little.

No footprints were evident other than her own today, so Carla knew she would be alone up here. Holding her breath in anticipation, she opened the unlocked door and stepped inside.

No way.

Her chilly hands flew to her face as she gasped. Someone had been in here all right. Somehow, they had lugged a whole bunch of belongings up the trail to make themselves at home.

The woodsy, musty smell was the same, but now, blue checked curtains hung at the windows, and an open shelf was stacked with pre-packaged provisions. A small propane heater was a new addition, and a table sat in the corner with two wooden chairs, not the rickety old plastic chairs she and her sister used to perch on. An old-fashioned lantern sat in the middle of the table, surrounded by books. Stacks of them, and a typewriter. Who even used a typewriter anymore? Someone, obviously. Because paper was threaded into it, and several paragraphs were already typed.

Carla hesitated in the doorway. She felt like she was in someone else's little house. Intruding. Yet, this was public property, she knew that much. The original structure had been here forever, and her dad always warned that one day they could find the place vandalized or even torn down. But this? Surreal. Who loved this place as much as she did?

Five years had passed since her last visit to her shack haven. New people had moved in around the lake, and anyone could come up here from Hollybrook. This spot was an inspirational slice of solitude. Peaceful. Picturesque. Private. If a person needed to get away from the distractions of everyday life, this location was ideal. Especially if their work required concentration and focus. For someone like a writer or a student perhaps.

Her fingers twitched as she looked over at the typewriter. Could she be that nosy? Would reading what was typed on that paper be classed as an invasion of privacy when the door wasn't locked, and as far as she knew, this was public property?

She pulled the door shut behind her and stepped into the center of the hut. The one room was small. Maybe fifteen feet by ten feet. Whoever used this place to work or study or whatever made good use of the space. She eyed the selection of food. Mainly snacks of the non-perishable variety. Packages of chocolate chip cookies, crackers, chips. A large jar of salsa and a couple of water jugs. Not exactly nourishing but perhaps sustaining enough if a person happened to be caught up here for a while. Or was working on some secret project...

She couldn't resist. Her bookish tendencies overpowered her sensible conscience. She had to know what that project was, even if it ended up being some boring school assignment or university paper. The books piqued her interest. Some were ancient with faded covers and gold lettering with unfamiliar titles. She cringed at the thought of books getting damaged by a leaky roof or by being dropped in the snow, but surely, their owner was coming back for them soon. Especially if they were a writer and lover of books.

A quick glance through the window confirmed she was still alone, and nobody would be walking in on her moment of curiosity. A pang of guilt reminded her she was supposed to be praying. And she would, as soon as she'd taken a quick peek at the papers on the table.

Sitting in the straight-legged wooden chair, she cocked her head to one side to read the titles of several newer books stacked in a neat pile. Contemporary thrillers. All by the same author, Riley Tomkins. *Never heard of him.* Although by the covers, they were a little gruesome for her taste. Maybe she didn't want to read what was written on the typewriter, after all.

A slim album at the bottom of the book stack caught her eye. A photograph album, perhaps. She slid it from beneath the novels, taking great care to leave the rest how she found them. Yes, definitely a photo album. She pursed her lips. *What do we have here?* Some clues about the writer? Her gaze landed on the tall pile of plain paper and array of sharp pencils. Was this person a fan of Riley Tomkins or could this be Mr. Tomkins's writing space?

The album. Carla inspected the burgundy cover and opened it. This was like the albums her mom used to keep with the clear sticky pages that held the pictures in place. On the first leaf, a class photo took up the whole space with "Hollybrook Middle School" printed along the bottom. Based on the dreadful hairstyles, this was about the same era as when she'd attended. She pushed her glasses farther up the bridge of her nose and did a double take. She saw her younger self in the front row comprising Mrs. Bennett's sixth grade students. Pigtails. Glasses. Skinny. What were the chances?

She turned the page to find several more class pictures. Some a couple of years apart but all typical poses—all tinged yellow—with everyone awkward and always with her in the front row since she was one of the shortest. A decent number of her fellow students had gone through school together, but was this whole album full of class photos?

Carla continued, page after page, into the high school years, and then her breath caught in her throat. Her grade twelve school portrait. Head and shoulders. The good ones they had done professionally by the school, and then the family ended up with so many that the students would hand them out to friends. She ran her finger over her face in the picture. She'd hardly changed in the almost decade since the photo was taken. Her hair was longer, and her skin had improved. Why on earth was she featured in this person's album? Maybe she would find more random portraits of her friends.

The next page. Only her. This time at a church potluck when she was home from university on a Christmas break.

NO.

Another page. At the lake with her sister. Bikinis. The year before she graduated.

And another. At a table inside the library. Reading. Her last summer in Hollybrook.

She dropped the album onto the table, and she covered her mouth with her hand as a sound escaped. Part scream, part sob.

The rest of the album held no other photos of her classmates. The only face looking up at her was her own.

Pages and pages, every one of them filled with shots of a younger Carla James.

The final one was snapped days before Rhys left her. She was outside the cabin, hammer in hand, attempting to fix the porch railing. Before her entire life fell apart.

Chapter Ten

A TREMOR RAN THROUGH CARLA'S BODY from her dizzy head to her frozen toes. She clutched the arms of the chair. Who was the photographer? Was he or she the same person who was working in this hut? Other than the album, no other personal effects were on the table. What was her connection to them? She eyed the stack of disturbing novels again. Sinister didn't begin to describe this scenario.

I need to go home.

Yet, her gut told her to gather as much information as she could. She was not coming back here again. Hoping for some kind of clue, she scanned the half-typed page threaded into the typewriter.

Her eyes raced across the paper:

Nobody would stand in his way. Not now. Not ever.

Her heart belonged to him, he made sure of that. He left his mark on her five years ago when she was his for the taking. The bond they had was eternal.

"She came back for me after all these years. Home for Christmas."

He watched her every move.

He was captivated. She was captive.

He raced down the mountain, snow spewing in his wake. He knew she would come home. Now she would be his... forever.

Her stomach roiled. What? The attack five years ago. Those photographs. This was all about her.

But only Alexis knew, and now Madison and Rhys.

She rubbed her aching temples. Plus, the attacker, of course.

Had the monster written these words? Sat in this chair?

Nausea rose from the pit of her belly.

She studied the pile of books. Riley Tomkins.

R.T.

The initials were R.T.

Like Rhys Templeton.

No…

Breathe. She inhaled and took in as much air as her lungs would allow. Then let out her breath slowly.

"I'm going crazy. This can't be right. It's a coincidence. That's all." Tears blurred her vision of the wretched typewriter. Rhys?

Water. *I need water.* She slid her backpack from her shoulders to the floor, delved inside for the water bottle, and chugged half the contents in the hope it would help her think clearly.

Lord, get me home.

The thought of the cabin reminded her of the footprints on the back porch, and the hair on the back of her neck prickled. Could Rhys have made those prints, after all? He was up at the cabin both nights, but his life was in Seattle now. This made no sense.

She attempted to stand, and her thigh brushed against a drawer she hadn't noticed before. Part of the table. As much as she wanted to get out of there, the drawer might hold answers to the unthinkable questions crowding her mind. Her pulse raced as she tugged on the small iron latch. Stuck. The drawer wasn't locked, but it must be warped. With both hands, she pulled hard, and it flew open. More plain paper. She lifted the empty pages, glad to not have the temptation to read more of his words—whoever *he* was— and dumped them on the tabletop, no longer caring about being neat and tidy.

She peered farther inside the drawer. "No, Rhys, no." She whispered his name.

Tucked at the back was the glass snowflake paperweight she'd planned on giving him the last Christmas they were together. Her hand flew to her mouth. How had he found the paperweight? That whole day was a blur of pain and fear—she couldn't recall where she'd put it. Had she left the gift under the tree for him? She lifted the snowflake out of its hiding place and held its denseness in the palm of her trembling hand, confused beyond all reason.

And as she looked back into the drawer gaping wide like an open mouth, a pack of winter mints rolled into sight, mocking her, and confirming she had found her assailant. Whoever that may be.

Rhys arrived at the lakeside cabin and killed the engine.

Was this another huge mistake, arriving unannounced to speak with Carla after last night's engagement revelation? If only he'd had the opportunity to explain before she'd shown him the door. Perhaps now. He ran his fingers over his stubbly jaw.

"I can only try."

He checked his phone—noon. Hopefully, Carla had experienced a good night's sleep and was feeling refreshed and willing to talk. Again. The groan of his rental car door echoed his heart as he pushed it open.

Before he could exit the vehicle, Madison appeared at the front door of the cabin. Her distraught face caused his stomach to knot.

He jumped out and jogged over to her. "Madison? What's wrong?"

"It's Carla. I may be overreacting, but she went snowshoeing on her own." She glanced at her phone. "Half an hour ago. I can't get any reply on her phone."

He exhaled. "Okay. Well, it's not unusual for the cell reception to be spotty up here, and if she's gone a good distance, there's little chance she'll have any at all, especially if she's in the forest area."

"Right." Madison crossed her arms. "I don't know, Rhys. I have a bad feeling, and there's not a thing I can do about it." She looked toward the lake. "I've never snowshoed in my life, and I wouldn't know where to go anyway."

Rhys narrowed his eyes as he scanned the trail along the lakeshore. "She didn't say where she was heading, I suppose? There are a few different routes she could have taken."

"I know she started at the lake. Went out the front door and locked it. She mentioned a shack?"

"The warming shed. That has to be the one she took me to several times." His heart skipped as he recalled their deep conversations and deeper kisses in that shed.

"Right." Madison's face lit up. "Must be the one. She said she was going to find this little shack because she wanted to pray about… some things."

"Oh." His shoulders slumped. "I presume she told you about our conversation last night?"

"Not much. Only that you're engaged."

"That's what I need to speak to her about. It's complicated."

"Love usually is." She smiled.

He felt his ears burn hot.

"I see the way you watch her. But for now, I'm concerned for her safety." She checked her phone again. "What if she's fallen or is hurt?"

"Or she may simply be enjoying the trails without even realizing there's no cell service and that you're worried about her—it's way warmer today, and she knows this area like the back of her hand." He slid out his own phone and passed it to Madison. "Although, I must admit, I'm a little rattled that she's out there alone after those footprints on her back porch the other night. Can you put your number in my contacts here? I don't mind going to check on her. In fact, I want to go. I have to speak with her anyway."

Madison tapped in her number. "Thanks. Do you remember how to get to the shack?"

"I do." He pictured the tiny structure in a clearing. "I'm fairly sure there's only one trail up there." He led the way to the cabin. "If memory serves, I think there should be some large sized snowshoes in the closet. Mind if I take a look?" He held the front door open for her.

"Be my guest. I'll grab you a couple of water bottles." She disappeared toward the kitchen as Rhys began rifling through the closet beneath the staircase. A gray backpack. Large snowshoes. Bingo.

"Oh, Carla will kill me for telling you, but I should mention something." Her voice carried through the living room. "She saw more boot prints in the snow on the back porch last night."

He straightened with the snowshoes in hand. "Excuse me?"

Madison's pinched face came into view. "Yeah. I saw them myself." She handed over the water bottles.

His heart hammered in his chest. "Really?"

"Nothing new this morning, and because it snowed even more overnight, any tracks beyond the porch were covered. That's disturbing though, isn't it?"

"It is. Please, lock up after I leave, and maybe give Alexis a call." He stuffed the bottles in the backpack. No time to search for gloves or a hat. He zipped up his jacket and hitched the backpack over his shoulders.

"She's on her way to pick up Lily. I'll fill her in."

"Thanks. I'll keep my phone on, so let's stay in touch. As well as possible in the mountains. Try not to worry. I'm sure everything's fine."

Within minutes, Rhys was on the trail that took him past the frozen lake and up the slope toward the wooded area. He rubbed his hands together as he walked. They'd soon warm up if he set a decent pace. The brooding clouds threatened more snow but not enough had fallen to cover another set of snowshoe tracks, which had to belong to Carla. Oh, Carla…

He'd forgotten how peaceful this area was. Other than two golden retrievers playing outside one of the other lakeside cabins and a red truck leaving the intimate community, everything was quiet. Even though his pulse thrummed a tinge of dread at the thought of Carla being in distress. Why had she gone so far from the cabin on her own after being freaked out by those footprints? Could the draw of that old shack have been so strong? That place used to be her favorite spot to pray. Prayer had always been important to Carla. One of the many things he loved about her.

Loved?

Yes, loved. What a predicament he'd managed to get himself into. Rather than spiral and dwell on the way he used to deal with stress, he prayed as he powered along the trail.

"Father, please be with Carla wherever she is. Help me to be able to find her and bring her home safe and sound. Lord, I'm sorry I've hurt two women." He winced. "Gabriella did nothing to deserve this, and I know she'll be okay because she has You. She's strong. Her faith is real. She was the one who encouraged me to meet up with Carla and make amends, wasn't she? Did she have an inkling that my feelings for Carla ran deeper than I cared to admit? That when I spoke about Carla, my heart ached? Maybe she did suspect. But I had no intention of causing her pain, Lord."

He gritted his teeth. When he phoned Gabriella late last night, she had cried. By the end of the conversation, she assured him he was doing the right thing.

"I had to be honest, Father. I had to let Gabriella go. She deserves a man with a whole heart to give. If there's any chance whatsoever for me with Carla, I need all the time I can get before she leaves for Mexico."

He stopped for a moment and leaned over his knees to catch his breath after a steep incline. He wasn't used to this. Five years ago, he could handle such physical exertion without breaking a sweat. Maybe praying out loud was using up too much oxygen. He certainly hadn't done much praying back in the day, but things were different now. He was a changed man. And he relied on God for His strength.

Time to keep focused and stay on track.

He gave his head a shake and continued through a heavily treed stretch, calling Carla's name in case she was injured or stuck somewhere. He shivered as the sun was now an absent friend, and he scanned either side of the trail for any signs of her. Was she okay? She'd been here, he was certain. At least one pair of tracks, maybe two that had gone before him. This was the most straightforward way to reach the shack. He swallowed down a lump of guilt when he pictured her up there praying. Was she praying for direction? For him to leave her alone so she could get on with her life? For grace to forgive him… again.

His phone rang, and he stopped mid-stride to slide it from his coat pocket.

"Madison?"

"Oh, I wasn't expecting to actually reach you. Yes, listen, something strange has happened."

"I'm not sure how long I'll have you on the line, so you'll have to talk fast." He blocked his other ear to hear better.

"Your tires. They're all flat. Slashed. Alexis arrived and spotted it straight away."

The line was patchy. "You say my tires have been slashed?" He frowned. Who had something against him?

"Yes. Alexis called the police. Something's off. Please be careful, and bring Carla back quick."

His stomach dropped. He stared out at the silent forest blanketed in white. No one else was up here. "I'm about halfway to the shack. I'll call when I can. Lock up and stay safe."

"We will. Don't worry about us. Take care, Rhys. I'm praying."

"Me, too."

With a renewed sense of urgency, he stashed the phone back in his coat pocket and increased his pace, praying with every step as snowflakes meandered through the trees.

Someone was playing twisted games, and their next move was anyone's guess.

Chapter Eleven

GOD, I DON'T KNOW WHAT TO do. Not one bone in my body wants to believe Rhys had anything to do with my attack. Surely, this is a huge mistake, Lord, surely?

Carla struggled to take the next breath, and her chest ached as tears spilled down her cheeks. She closed her eyes and tried to relive that horrific experience of her attack, to prove she was wrong. It took several seconds to recall details, since with counselling, she'd worked hard to erase those memories after endless nightmares and skittish behavior around men.

The antiseptic-like smell of winter mints. The strength and bulk of the man knocking her to the floor of the back porch. The clatter of broken rocking chairs as she struggled. His meaty hand covering her mouth and silencing her screams. A shudder slithered through her body.

Her eyes flew open, certain of one thing—her attacker was not Rhys. How could she even have suspected him? She would have known if he had been the one. The man was bigger, bulkier, taller than Rhys's six-foot frame, and his hand was… rough. The skin dry like sandpaper. Rhys was not afraid of hard work, but back then, his hands were more used to kitchen duties, and she'd teased him mercilessly about his insistence on using hand cream after being on dishwashing duty. His hands were… lovely. Besides, he had no reason to attack her. She would have married the man that day if he'd only asked.

She stood and paced like a caged lion. Could he have arranged for someone else to attack her? She squeezed her fingers around the paperweight. No, again, absolutely zero reason to do so.

Then who? And why?

A muffled sound outside brought her back to the moment, and she froze. Had the writer—her attacker—come to work on his story? *Her* story? Panic flooded through her veins, and she clutched the paperweight tighter. She would use it as a missile if necessary because she had nowhere to hide. Her pulse pounded in her ears as she slid up against the shack wall, behind the door. Perhaps she could surprise him.

My snowshoes. He would see them leaning against the front steps, but he wouldn't know they belonged to Carla, would he? The snowshoes could belong to anyone…

"Carla?"

Rhys caught his breath as he entered the clearing. The old shack was exactly as he remembered. The embodiment of rustic.

"Carla." His lungs screamed, and his voice was hoarse after calling for her in the forest. He'd drained one water bottle and was determined to save the other for Carla when he eventually found her. He *would* find her. He plodded on toward the shack.

The snow had been falling steadily for some time, but he followed two sets of tracks that looked relatively fresh. At least in the past twenty-four hours. Both led to the entrance. He was no expert, but one set looked more like the indents made by cross-country skis. Only those appeared to have travelled back out. Strange.

"Carla?" he called out again.

Where were her snowshoes? If she'd been here already, she could have gone back home by another route. Not that he could recall another one—but she knew this area way better than he did. His heart sank. Unless her snowshoes were around the back for some reason. Or she'd taken them inside. Only one way to find out.

Rhys checked his phone. No new messages, and one tiny bar promising hope of a signal. He'd check in as soon as he had some news for the ladies waiting in the cabin. He bent over and unlatched his snowshoes. With light feet and an anxious knot in his gut, he hurried up the steps and pushed open the door.

The next second, the door slammed shut, hitting him square in the face, and knocked the wind right out of him. He shook his head and blinked. *What just happened?*

"Carla? Are you in here? It's me. Rhys."

The door opened an inch at a time until Carla stood before him, her eyes puffy from crying, and her face as white as the snow on the ground.

"What happened?" He stepped inside the shack and wrapped her in a hug, inhaling the light floral scent that reminded him of oranges. Her rigid body shook with silent sobs, and he stroked her back with care. This woman felt as if she might shatter into pieces at any moment, her fists balled in front of her chest. Carla was so strong. So sure. Had *he* done this to her? He assessed the shack as she trembled in his arms. Someone seemed to be using it as some kind of office. Who would come all the way up here to work?

Something dug into his ribs. Was she clutching a pointed object in her hands? He eased back to see her face so they could talk. Her glasses had fogged up, and he slid them from her nose to look into her chocolate-brown eyes. They were haunted. Scared. Was she upset about the footprints back at the cabin?

"Rhys, we need to get out of here." She raised her shaky voice, and her chin trembled. Something had spooked her, for sure.

"Can you tell me what's going on?" He nodded at the glass in her hands. "What's that?"

"A paperweight. It's a snowflake, something I bought to give you on our last Christmas…"

Snowflake. They had a special thing with snowflakes. He swallowed down the memory. But why was the ornament here?

"You brought it up with you?" This could be part of her praying about everything. Letting go of the past.

"No. I found it in that drawer." She nodded toward the desk where a small drawer lay open.

"I'm a bit confused here. Can you explain?" He kept his voice calm and as gentle as possible.

She nodded, wiping her cheeks with the back of her jacket sleeve. "I'll try. Honestly, I think we should leave. We need to call the police. This is my attacker's hideout."

"Your attacker?" The word lodged in his throat. "You mean from… that Christmas Eve? How do you know?"

"I can explain on our way down." She took her glasses back, slipped them on, and eyed his backpack. "First, let me grab the evidence. We can fit it in our packs. Do you have your phone? Is there service up here?"

He put his hands on her shoulders. "Whoa. Slow down for a second. Madison already called the police. They're probably on their way to the cabin, or they could already be there."

"Good." She didn't even ask why but straightened and lifted her chin. "Rhys, this guy has been stalking me for years. He knows I'm home for Christmas. And… and he wants me." Her bottom lip wobbled. "He could show up here any minute. I need to take a few things with us."

Her organizational skills were showing, and she was taking charge, even in her fragile state.

Rhys passed his backpack over to her. "Here, fill it up."

"Thanks." She slid a pile of books inside. "You try to get hold of Madison. Tell her we're leaving and should be there in an hour, tops." She slipped her own backpack onto a chair and unzipped it. Repositioning a water bottle to the side pocket, she picked up the snowflake paperweight and tucked it inside her pack.

Rhys took out his phone. "Good. I actually have bars on this thing." Whatever was going on, they needed to make contact with Madison or Alexis. Get help.

Carla didn't answer but grabbed paper from an old typewriter, and then a roll of mints from an open drawer. Curious. She stuffed them into her pack with trembling fingers.

Madison answered.

"Hey, Madison. I'm at the old shack. I have Carla. We should be home around two o'clock."

"Rhys? You're breaking up…"

He spoke louder and moved closer to the window. "Carla is okay, but we need the police. She's found something." *I'm not sure what exactly.*

"Police? Did you say police? Oh, Rhys, this is a bad line. The police are about five minutes out. Alexis…"

"Hello?" He pulled the phone away from his ear. The call had ended. He let out a growl of frustration. "It's super spotty up here. We may have more luck outside in the clearing. Are you ready to go?" He may not know the details yet, but obviously Carla didn't feel safe in this shack, and the sooner she was back at her cabin, the better. Especially if they could persuade the police to meet with them.

"Rhys, can I use your phone quick to take a few snaps? Mine is dead."

"Of course."

He watched as she methodically documented what was left on the desk.

She shuddered, handed him back the phone, and slid into her backpack. "Done. Let's go."

"Are your snowshoes out back?" He fastened his pack and shouldered it.

"Back? No, they're outside on the steps. You walked right past them when you came in."

Oh no. "Carla, there were no snowshoes outside. I wasn't sure you were even in here. It's deserted."

"They have to be there." Her eyes widened. She rushed to the front door and rattled the knob. She turned, and her face crumpled. "Rhys, we're locked in."

Chapter Twelve

Was he out there watching? Waiting? Carla's skin prickled.

"It's locked? What on earth?"

Carla stood back and watched as Rhys tried manhandling the doorknob, to no avail. He let out a groan.

She peered through the front window from one side, afraid of what she might see. "There's nobody out there," she whispered. A glance at the porch steps. "There are no snowshoes either." Nausea curdled her stomach as she realized how close this man had been, and she hadn't heard a thing.

"Mine are gone, too?" He joined her, putting an arm around her trembling shoulders. "Who *is* this guy?"

"More to the point, what are we going to do?" She wrung her hands. "He knows we're both inside. Even if we got out through a window, he has our snowshoes, so we can't take off down that steep incline. The snow's too deep, especially if we're being chased." She spun around to face him. "Can you check your phone again?"

"Sure." He held his phone up in the air, as if that might actually help. "Nope. Nothing. Madison knows I'm with you. I think she heard when I said we were at the shack."

"She definitely heard we needed the police." Carla checked the back window. A clearing led to snowy trees and more snowy trees.

"They're not likely to send a search team for at least an hour. They think we're making our way down to the cabin."

The cabin. A deep longing for the place caused her eyes to brim. She blinked back more tears. "So, we stay put. What if this guy wants to hurt us? Hurt me?" Flashes of that fateful night ran through Carla's brain, and panic clouded her thoughts. *Please God, no.*

Rhys blew out a long stream of air and paced the cramped area, his fingers raking through his thick hair. "Let's think about this logically. You said he wants you now that you're back home in Hollybrook. How do you know?"

"It's here, on paper." She dropped her backpack to the floor and dug out the sheets of paper. "See?" She handed him the page. "I think he's an author." She pointed to the desk. "Those are his books. Dark thrillers."

He scanned the paragraph. "Wow. Then I don't think he'll want to kill you. Not if he wants you." He returned the page to her pack.

"What about *you*?"

He rubbed his chin. "With my tires being slashed, I think his message is clear."

"What? Your tires?"

"Madison called when I was halfway up here to say someone had slashed my tires outside the cabin."

"Could he have had time to do that and then get back up the trail?" Unless he had some sort of snowmobile, but they would have heard the motor. This secluded spot was as quiet as a graveyard.

"No, but it can't be a coincidence. Maybe he has an accomplice or something." A muscle in his jaw popped.

"An accomplice?" Her voice broke at the thought of a gang of men.

Rhys checked his phone. "I'll keep my eye on this. As soon as there's a hint of service, I'll get a call in to Madison." Worry laced his eyes.

Carla was no fool; she wasn't the only one feeling the fear. She bit a thumbnail and glared out into the clearing of white nothingness at the front of the shack, careful to stay out of plain sight. "So, we sit here and wait?" For help… or for the lunatic to make his next move.

Rhys leaned against the table and folded his arms across his chest. "I could break us out of here—but we don't know what's waiting outside. Better to stall for time and pray that the police come looking for us. If he's alone, between the two of us, we may have a chance. Especially if we can figure out what makes this guy tick." He picked up one of the books on the table. "Riley Tomkins. I'm presuming you don't know him?"

She shook her head. "I want to get out of here. It's giving me the creeps. If we're stuck inside, we should brainstorm. Figure it out. Meanwhile, I'll keep watch through the back window, and you watch through the front. That way, if we catch even a glimpse…"

"Sure." He scoured the small room and grabbed a broom from the corner. "Not much in the way of worthy weapons, but take this."

She raised her brows.

"Go for his eyes."

Squished eyeballs? She squirmed but accepted the broom and took her post at the back window. "This Riley Tomkins, or whatever his real name is—I'm thinking this is a nom de plume—he knew me when I was young."

"He did? How do you figure?"

"In your backpack there's a photo album along with the novels. Lots of school class pictures, that sort of thing. I'm in every one of them. The other photos are only of me. My high school graduation. Me home from university on breaks. Right up to the last winter when you and I were up at the cabin." She gritted her teeth. "It's horrifying to think he was watching me when I didn't know."

"I'm sorry, Carla. This guy… I can't imagine the terror…." He was quiet for several beats. "So, he must have carried on his sick crush when you came back from university?"

"I think so." She licked her lips. "Even while you and I were dating. Somehow, he knew you left on that Christmas Eve, and that I was alone." She watched fragile snowflakes floating to the ground with such grace, a sheer contrast to the horror of past memories and the crushing fear of the present. "I feel so helpless."

She felt Rhys's arms around her waist. His chin rested on her shoulder. She closed her eyes and took solace in the brief moment of comfort. Then, she snapped her eyes open. They were supposed to be looking out for a maniac. And Rhys was engaged to be *married*. This was all so wrong.

She shrugged him away and pointed at the front window with the broom. "Go. He must be watching. Or waiting."

"Right. I just… it feels like we still have so much to talk about." He sighed as he retreated to his post. "Yes, this Riley Tomkins. Anyone in school by the name of Riley?"

"Not that I can remember. I can't think of anyone who was into writing specifically. A bunch of us were nerdy and hung out at the library a lot." *Who could it be?* "Most went away to study, some stayed behind. I didn't really keep in close contact with any of my friends when I went to Vancouver. You know how it is, we all change."

"The things you thought were deathly important in high school are inconsequential."

"Exactly." She peered out to the patch of trees beyond a pristine stretch of snow. *Was he watching from there?*

"What if I try to break down the door? I could even smash a window. See what he's playing at."

"Rhys, we don't know how dangerous he is. He could have a gun. Or there could be two or more of them."

"Then *what* are they waiting for?" He smacked the wall.

She whipped her head around.

He stood with his back to her, staring through the window, his hands scraping through his hair. "I'm going crazy here. What on *earth* is he doing?"

Carla walked over and touched his back. "He could be waiting for this. For one or both of us to crack and run out there into the clearing." She gestured to the shelves lined with snacks. "We can wait him out. He doesn't know you have a phone and got through to Madison. That she already called the police."

"I suppose it's not too cold in here. I can see if the propane heater works." His forehead wrinkled. "How are you not freaking knowing he's lurking out there?"

She plucked her almost empty water bottle from the side pocket of her pack and drained it. Plenty more were stacked on the shelf. "I'm freaking out on the inside, but I'm also praying with almost every breath. I don't know for sure, but I can't help thinking he's biding his time. Waiting for you to go for help? Or for us both to attempt to leave without our snowshoes."

He handed her a freshwater bottle from the shelf before returning to his window, and she went back to hers. "He knows there's no way we could outrun him if he has snowshoes. Or cross-country skis. Or a snowmobile."

She narrowed her eyes as she peered out at the rear of the property. A squirrel caught her attention as it scurried up the trunk of one of the tallest trees and out of sight. If only they could get away so easily. "I don't think anyone could ride a snowmobile all the way through the forest. Unless he came the other way from town, but even that's risky."

She heard Rhys chug water. "Okay. So, our best option is that we stay here and hope the police come before he gets antsy and blasts his way in."

"That could take, what—another two hours? Unless the authorities came the long way with a snowmobile."

"Providing Madison and Alexis persuade them we're in need of help."

Carla pursed her lips. "Alexis knows most of the police force personally. I think she could call in some favors, if necessary."

"Good. Let's hope so. Our other option is for me to take a chance and get outside to make an emergency call if I can get bars on this wretched phone. There's no way I'm leaving you alone in this place while I attempt to get help. We'd have to go together."

"Without snowshoes."

"Yeah." He groaned. "I'm not loving our chances."

Carla tapped her chin. "There is a third option." She worked the plan through in her mind.

"I'm listening."

"What if you break out the front door and pretend like you're making a run for it. If he's out there watching, he'll know I'm alone. He'd come in and expect me to be here all vulnerable, but instead, we've set some sort of trap to catch him. You come back and surprise him. Tie him up. Lock him back in here if we have to. If help still isn't here, we make our way down—our snowshoes have to be out there somewhere."

"It might work…" He shook his head. "There are so many things that could go wrong."

"Such as?" She set a hand on one hip.

"Why would he think I'd be fool enough to leave you up here alone?"

"I don't know. I can't guess how this madman's mind works." She straightened her toque and focused on the snow still falling from the sky. *Think. Think.* "I've got it." She turned to him. "Let's stage a fight. A huge argument. Make it realistic."

"Hmm. That might convince him I was willing to leave you by yourself, I guess. What if he comes in here with a weapon? He could have a gun, a knife, anything. And he could easily overpower you." He left the window, and they met in the middle of the space. Pain etched his face. He didn't need to say the word *again.* They were thinking the same thing. "You could simply freeze on the spot. It would be understandable."

"Then let's make the trap airtight. Please, Rhys. He's a bad man. He needs to be caught." She took a deep breath and struggled to keep her composure. "I let him get away before." She bit out each word. "It's not happening this time. Do you understand?"

He blinked at her anguished tone, set his water bottle on the table, and then cupped her face in both his hands. "I understand. I'll do anything to keep you safe. I'm not going anywhere without you. I promise you that." Their noses were an inch apart.

Panic and passion collided as Carla's heart beat against her ribcage. Rhys was so close their breaths mingled, and she mustered every ounce of willpower not to kiss him. He cared. He cared for her safety, and maybe he loved her still somehow, even if he was engaged to someone else.

"What about Gabriella?" she whispered. "You're getting married. Why are you playing with my feelings like this?"

A sad smile curved his lips. "I'm not playing. Gabriella knows my heart. She's always known I was holding a piece back from her. The piece that belonged to you."

She still held a piece of his heart? Really? Carla cocked her head to one side. "But… but you proposed to her. You love each other."

"It's not that simple. It's been… rocky. She's been more than patient with me. With my commitment issues. I told her all about you from the beginning. What I did to you. When I told Gabriella you'd reached out after finding me through Madison's party plans, she suggested I meet with you. Kind of like putting out a fleece to see if there was anything still between us. She suspected I still loved you deep down. And she didn't want to be second best. We spoke last night, and she's called off the engagement. We're over."

"Oh." What was she supposed to say to that? Sorry? Definitely not…

"What I'm trying to say is, I want to give us another chance. You and me." He put one finger over her lips. "Shh. Don't say a word. This is not the ideal time or place. Before we do anything drastic with our outrageous plans to escape here, I had to tell you where I stand."

You stand very, very close to me. On impulse, she leaned in and planted a kiss on his lips. They were as delicious as she remembered.

He let out a gentle moan. "Was that a promise of what might be in our future?"

She took a step backwards, still clutching her water bottle. "I'll give it consideration once we're safe."

"And we *will* be safe." He checked his phone. "Almost one fifteen." He stared at the screen for a few more seconds. "You know, I don't see any help arriving until three thirty at the earliest. Not unless I can get another call in to Madison. They're expecting us to be on our way down and may not send help until two thirty."

"We can't sit here for another two hours. More to the point, we don't know if *he* can sit and wait that long in the snow."

"Although, it seems he's a patient man." Rhys wrinkled his nose. "He's been waiting for you for years. You'd think he would've given up hope when you left for Mexico."

"Maybe he did. Until he heard I was coming home for Christmas. Small town. Word gets around. He could even be married for all we know."

"Married?" Rhys began rifling through random items around the room. "Poor woman, if he is. This man's deranged."

"He needs help."

He stopped and looked over at her. "That's awfully generous of you."

"Grace. Forgiveness has a sister named Grace. Trust me, I haven't mastered it by any stretch of the imagination. I've read and learned a lot about it over the years."

"Did you also happen to read up about how to make weapons from junk by chance?" He held up a rusted metal bucket—but Carla spotted the treasure hidden behind it.

She grinned. "I think that beaver trap might be a good start."

A branch snapped from somewhere outside the back window, and they both dropped to the wooden floor. The treed area was at least twenty feet from the shack, but that sounded closer.

A trickle of sweat ran down Carla's back, and she lowered her voice to a whisper. "We need to work fast. He may not be as patient as we thought."

Chapter Thirteen

Rhys crept to the back window and inched his face as close as he dared without being spotted. This maniac knew they were both inside, but Rhys didn't like the idea of making himself a clear target, in case the guy did have a gun. They were proverbial sitting ducks.

His heart raced with the adrenaline rush, but he had to attempt cool, calm, and collected for Carla's sake, even though his heart rate begged to differ. He concentrated on keeping his voice even. "I can't see him. He may have gone around to the front."

A quick glance over his shoulder. Carla was already next to the front window, her back pressed against the wall as she rotated her head to peek outside.

A gasp.

"You see him?" In two strides, Rhys was by her side.

"A quick glimpse over there by that clump of smaller trees." She pointed a shaky finger to the right. "I don't think he can see us. Unless he has binoculars." She bit her lip. "Which he probably has, if he's been making a sport out of watching me."

Rhys scrunched his eyes closed. *I need to think clearly. Try to imagine what this guy is going to do next.*

"You okay?" Carla touched his arm.

"Yeah." He met her gaze. "Can you keep an eye on the spot where you last saw him? You should be able to tell if he moves from those trees. I'm going to figure out this beaver trap and hope it'll catch more than beavers."

"Mind your fingers." Carla wrinkled her nose. "Seriously, you need them all in your line of work." She turned back to the window. "I'll be over here watching and praying. If you hand me your phone, I'll keep checking for service."

"Sounds good." He passed his phone to her, set his backpack on the wooden floor, and focused on the contraption he'd dragged from the junk pile, along with a few extra supplies that might prove useful.

The trap was old. Rusty. Although he'd never set an actual beaver trap in his life, his mom had made him set mouse traps in the attic when he was a kid. He hated doing that but didn't have a choice. He was the eight-year-old man of the house when his dad left them. He'd learned to grow up quickly. Too quickly.

"I see him." Carla moved along the edge of the window and snapped several photos with his phone. "Now we have images, too."

"Good thinking. If we ever get a signal, we can send them to Madison. Is he coming closer?" Rhys maneuvered the sizable trap to the center of the shack where he had more room to set it. He took extra care, knowing a snap would be unforgiving.

"No. I can't tell what he's doing, but he's still at those trees. He could be on the phone. He's pacing. Wait, he's limping, I think. Hmm. There's something familiar…"

"Limping?" *If he's injured, that will work in our favor.*

He glanced over again to find Carla studying the phone, pinching the photo images to make them larger. "Beard. Tall. Black jacket, black snow pants. Can't see his face. He's got a dark toque on."

"How on earth would he get up here if he's injured? Unless he hurt himself once he arrived."

"Oh, my goodness." She clutched the phone to her chest. "He's not injured."

Rhys stood. "Then what?" He tilted his head.

All color drained from her face.

"Carla, what is it?"

"I think I know who he is. Can you keep watch a sec?" They traded places, and she delved into his backpack and pulled out the photo album. Laying it out on the table, she flicked through the pages. "There. There. And there." Her fear was palpable as she shuddered over the album.

"Tell me?"

"A guy I was in school with." She brought the book over to Rhys. "He's in all these class pictures. He was deathly shy. Smart. Loner. Picked on. I felt sorry for him, to be honest. He would hang out on the peripheral of our nerdy group. I always tried to be kind. I guess he took it as more."

"The limp?"

She nodded. "It didn't help the bullying issue. He had one leg a bit shorter than the other. I don't even know why. It didn't stop him from doing sports. Especially skiing. He was good at it." She covered her mouth with her hand. "This is all making sense now. Alexis said he married this really quiet girl. She cleans our cabin. I think he might be our… our handyman. They live at the lake, Rhys." A rogue tear trickled down her cheek. "We grew up as neighbors."

Rhys's jaw dropped. "Oh, man."

He'd been watching and waiting. Did his wife have a key to the cabin if she was a cleaner? How often had he been in the cabin? Rhys's gut wrenched every time he thought about what that violent monster did to Carla. What kind of man…

He straightened and looked over at the table. "So those gruesome books—he's a writer? He wrote those?"

"I guess so. I didn't know him well. Clearly. But Riley Tomkins is pretty close to his real name."

Rhys raised his brows and glanced down at her pale face.

"Richard. My attacker is Richard Tremblay."

Saying his name out loud was both empowering and sickening. After five years, she finally knew who her attacker was.

"You okay?" Rhys rested a hand on her shoulder and gave a gentle squeeze.

"Yeah. I'll keep watch here." She slammed the album shut, shoved it in the backpack, and resumed her surveillance through the front window. Was he watching her from the trees? Had he followed her to the restaurant yesterday? She'd looked into his eyes. They had pierced through her. The more she thought about those eyes, they'd been menacing. Not right.

Rhys stroked her hair with a feather light touch. "I'm so sorry, Carla. Sorry it was someone you knew. He's messed up. I hate that you're taking the brunt of it again for no reason."

"I guess we both are now, but you better carry on with that trap." She tried to recall an occasion where she'd given Richard reason to think they ever had a hope of even dating. Nothing. She hadn't dated seriously in high school anyway. Her dad had been strict about it, and she was a rule follower. Unlike Alexis. *I'll have to ask her if she can think why Richard would be doing this. If we ever get off this mountain.*

"He has to be thinking on the fly." Rhys moved away and began scraping something on the trap.

"True. He definitely wouldn't expect me to stumble across his lair with all the photos and everything."

"Unless he did." Rhys paused, then spoke again. "He could have known this was your special place. That's likely why he chose to write about you here. Poetic or something."

Carla swallowed down the taste of bile. "He wasn't expecting *you*."

"Right. He's not happy. My tires attest to that."

"But like we said, he couldn't have been in two places at once." She set her hands on her hips and pivoted to face him. "His wife? Do you think that little whip of a thing may have slashed your tires? Could she be in on this?" She gasped. "Surely not."

"We can't assume anything. She might not know how far he's willing to go. Or she might be caught in an abusive relationship with him. Who knows?"

She swiveled back to the window, her cheeks wet. Tears had leaked without her even knowing. "This has to stop. He has to be stopped. That beaver trap better work." Her pulse picked up speed. "Oh, Rhys, he's on the move. I see him. He's staying behind the trees, but he's heading this way. Getting closer."

Rhys came beside her, slipped an arm around her waist, and they both watched from the edge of the window. "This has to work. I don't see any obvious gun on him, but we can't be sure. As soon as I break out through the door, you need to slide that trap right in front of the entrance. Just be sure there's room for the door to swing in."

"Will the trap be enough?" Her heart thumped so hard she could feel the rhythmic thrum reverberate through her body. "What if it doesn't snap?" The thought of being alone with Richard was beyond terrifying.

"I'll come straight back. I promise." He turned her to face him and stroked her cheek with his thumb. "Whether the trap works or not, I'm not leaving you alone. We'll fight this together."

She gulped down fear and picked up his backpack. "Here. We should start arguing. Make it good. Take the phone, too. If you get bars on this thing, call Madison before you come back for me. They have to know what happened, just in case…"

He slipped the phone into his coat pocket and shouldered the backpack. "We're both going to be okay." He pressed his lips to hers, and time stopped for one moment of pure bliss. "You're one brave lady, Carla James. Pray with me?"

She bowed her head, and Rhys's deep voice washed over her.

"Father, we need You now more than ever. I pray You will protect Carla and that this man will be stopped. That justice will be served. That You would give Carla and me the strength we need both now and going forward. In Jesus's name. Amen."

"Amen." Her limbs trembled as she stared at the only man she had ever truly loved. This couldn't be the last time they would be together. "I can't bear the thought of anything happening to you out there, Rhys."

"Keep praying, my love. And now, let's fight like our lives depend on it."

God, help us. "I can't believe you came crawling back to me, Rhys. I will never take you back." She prayed the scream from her lips sounded authentic, because everything within her wanted to drag him close and never let him go.

"You're not worth the effort. I'm out of here. For good." His shouting was realistic. Shocking.

Carla flinched when he kicked the center of the door once, twice, and then the third time, it broke open.

"Keep your stupid cabin. This pathetic town is too small for me anyway." He threw the words over his shoulder loud enough that they should carry through the clearing.

Good job. "Goodbye, Rhys. Thanks for hollowing out my heart with your selfishness. Don't even think of coming back. We're over," she yelled into the frigid winter air and heard her voice echo back to her. Her heart clenched even though she was deep in acting mode. "I deserve someone who will never leave me. You hear?" Her voice broke on the last word.

Rhys turned back from the bottom of the porch steps. He heard all right. "I hear you. Goodbye, Carla."

Adrenaline pumped through her veins as she slammed the battered door behind him, breathless and spent. *God, please, keep him safe out there.*

With care, she slid the monstrosity of a trap closer to the door so it couldn't be missed or even jumped over. Hopefully, Richard would be so desperate to get inside, he'd only have eyes for her and not look down.

Now what? If all went as planned, Richard would come in all fires blazing and step into the beaver trap. Had she thought this through? Wouldn't he collapse across the entrance? Would he simply let her pass on her way out? And if the ancient trap didn't do its job thoroughly enough, she was in trouble.

She would be the one trapped instead.

Chapter Fourteen

Rhys stomped through the thick snow and stayed in character as he ranted to himself, hoping the stalker was watching the performance. He glanced back over his shoulder. No sign of any man. Snowflakes fell on the old shack with Carla tucked inside. On her own. *God, help her to be strong. Help me, too.*

Richard hadn't come out from his hiding place yet, so as much as Rhys wanted to run back and protect Carla, he needed to keep walking. Traversing the snow in regular boots was harder than he thought, each step sinking deep. If only he knew where their snowshoes were stashed. Maybe in that clump of trees where Richard had been hunkered down?

He checked his phone, and his heart leapt.

One bar lit up. Then two.

If he was going to call, he had to do so now before he reached the forest and trees blocked the signal.

"Rhys?"

"Madison." He spoke in a rough whisper. "Please listen carefully. We need help. Now. We are still at the shack. With Carla's attacker."

"What? Alexis is here with me. You're on speaker."

"Good. The guy is Richard Tremblay."

Alexis swore. "Is Carla okay?"

"I'm going back in for her now."

Madison gasped. "Rhys, what can we do?"

"Let the police know, and pray. I'll call when I can."

He slid the phone in his pocket and continued into the dense covering of trees. He had to look convincing if their plan had any hope of working.

Carla huddled in the corner of the room, the broom handle clutched in her fingers. The last she saw of Rhys through the window, he disappeared into the forest behind a veil of snowflakes, and she was now completely and utterly alone.

He will never leave you nor forsake you…

The precious Bible verse she had memorized settled deep in her heart. She wasn't alone. God was with her now and always would be. He promised never to forsake her, never to break her heart, never to hurt her soul. He was her one true hope. If none of her sweet dreams and perfect plans for an ideal future came to pass, she would be okay because she would still have her Heavenly Father to love and guide her. That would never change. He would never change.

She squeezed her eyes shut. "God, I trust You. Thank You for being here with me in this moment. For promising to never leave. But I'm scared, and I need Your help. Give me wisdom. And please let the beaver trap do its thing and protect me from this maniac."

The one who had wrecked the better part of her early twenties. She took slow, intentional breaths, in and out in an attempt to silence the fear, frustration, and feral desire to give this man what he deserved.

The seconds ticked by. What was he waiting for? She was fit to burst.

Daughter, let it all out.

The whisper to her soul caught her by surprise. Cry. She should cry not only to release the pressure that built within her like a shaken bottle of champagne, but she should also cry to play along with the charade of the massive fight with the man she once loved. She corrected herself. *No, I still love him. I can't pretend otherwise.*

With all the pent-up emotions long locked away, she let everything out in deep, dramatic sobs. The wailing felt like healing. She'd never cried out like this before, let go completely, holding nothing back. First, for the love lost when Rhys left her rejected and alone with a mere note. And then, for the violent cruelty Richard Tremblay had inflicted upon her for no reason other than his own deranged disillusions.

She allowed foul words to pour from her mouth, ridding the hidden part of herself of the pain Richard had caused. Kind, nice, Carla—the one who always had encouraging words to share and a generous spirit—now allowed the dam to burst wide open. Yes, let the awful man hear her raw emotions. She cried for the years she had spent afraid of all men. For the security and safety, she had worked so hard to rebuild in her life. For the unknown future that lay before her. For the sheer terror of what could happen in the next minutes or hours…

He crashed through the door.

Carla's cries silenced instantly as his desperate eyes bore a hole into her very soul, and then in a split second, she witnessed him take a stride toward her—and into the open jaws of the iron trap.

A sickening snap.

A roar rose out of his bearded mouth, and he twisted onto the floor. He dropped whatever he'd been carrying and clutched both hands—those meaty hands—around his leg and writhed in pain.

Moments blurred. Her screams. His growls. The broom handle in her hands beating down on him over and over and over.

Until he grabbed one end and yanked her toward him, the sudden jolt sending her glasses flying across the room. He grabbed her forearms with a vice-grip.

Her shriek pierced her own ears.

Where was Rhys? He was coming back for her. She knew he would. He loved her.

Blood oozed from the mangled ankle above Richard's boot, and the putrid metallic scent filled the air. She caught a glimpse of white. Bone.

She struggled to escape his clutches, but he was strong. She was only now remembering how strong. But the broom was strewn beside her, and Rhys's words echoed in her mind.

With one almighty tug, she pulled one hand free, reached the middle of the stick, and as Richard tugged her back toward him, the end of the broom slammed into his eye socket.

He bellowed and released her as both hands flew to his face.

Now. She sprung up and straight into Rhys's broad chest. "Rhys."

He propelled her away from the bloody mess and toward the open door.

She watched from the entrance as Rhys took a gunny sack from under the table and threw it over Richard's head. With no regard for Richard's broken leg still mangled in the trap, Rhys rolled him over onto his stomach and stuck his knee in the man's back. She let out a cry.

Rhys looked up at Carla. "You hurt?"

She shook her head. No words would come, and her entire body was numb.

"Good." He knelt harder, and Richard expelled a groan. "Now to tie him up."

She hadn't noticed the length of rope before, and with some fancy twists and knots, Rhys had those monstrous hands bound in no time.

Richard moaned in agony. He wasn't going anywhere. The animal had been trapped.

Rhys removed his own scarf and worked with nimble fingers as he made a tourniquet and tied it around the man's leg. She wasn't sure she would have been as generous, but something about Rhys's actions stirred her heart.

"You are a coward and a sick, sick man." Rhys bent over the sack. "You don't deserve to live after what you did to Carla, but I'm going to make sure justice is served. The world will be a better place with you behind bars." His menacing tone caused Carla to shiver. But his protective stance sent a warmth that spread from her belly to her toes and her fingertips.

She blew out a long, slow breath. "It's over."

Rhys nodded. "It's over."

"And you came back."

"I promised I would never leave you again. I meant it." He reached for her glasses on the floor and stood. "Let's go home?" He slid them onto her nose and kissed her forehead. "Unless you want to wait it out up here until the authorities arrive?"

She looked down at her pathetic attacker as he rocked from side to side, low groans coming from within the sack. Should she say something to him? Ask him why? Why her?

No. She would not give him the satisfaction of having a conversation. No excuse was acceptable for what he had done to her—and what else he had done to others. Even his wife.

"I don't want to stay here a second longer." She turned from her attacker and looked into Rhys's kind hazel eyes, their golden flecks warm and welcoming.

"I was hoping you'd say that." He squeezed her hand. "Our snowshoes are outside. They were with his cross-country skis and a stash of other stuff in the trees. I grabbed them on my way back."

"Thank goodness."

"He's not moving anytime soon. I'll make another call so they send paramedics, maybe the long way up on snowmobiles or whatever they use."

Carla rubbed her arms where they'd been squeezed. Her head pounded, her eyes were scratchy from crying, and a blanket of exhaustion weighed heavy on her shoulders, but she lifted her chin. "Let's get going. Downhill is easier. All I need is to be back in my cabin with people I love."

He held the battered door open as she passed through. "Any chance I might have an invite, too?" His eyes pleaded.

She plodded down the steps of the old shack and strapped her snowshoes over her boots.

Rhys followed suit, and silence stretched between them as snowflakes fell like confetti.

"Actually, Rhys,"—a flirty smile curved her lips for the first time in forever—"I'd say you have an open-ended invitation."

Chapter Fifteen

"Almost home," Rhys spoke behind her as they paced in single file down the final descent to the frozen lake.

Carla's legs trembled, exhaustion clawed at every muscle, and fatigue washed over her body. "Can we take a break for a minute?"

"Sure." He stopped and passed the water bottle he'd carried ever since they handed their backpacks over to the authorities in the forest. "You going to make it to the cabin?"

She nodded as she drank. "Five minutes and we'll be there. I can do this."

Rhys took out his phone and tapped a message. "I'll ask Madison to run you a bath and make some hot chocolate."

"Sounds heavenly. Did I tell you about the amazing clawfoot tub?"

"You did. You really love this cabin, don't you?"

"It's always been special to me. Until over twenty years of good memories were marred by one Christmas Eve. It rocked my world in some ways. I lost my sense of home." Her gaze roamed the picturesque setting with cabins nestled along the shoreline. "In the same way that Alexis gave the old place a facelift, I see now I can replace the ugly moments from my past with beautiful ones in the present." She gave him the half empty bottle.

"I'd like to help with those beautiful moments." He put his hand over hers and didn't let go. "About that open-ended invitation you mentioned…"

The flutter of hope she felt earlier broke through her weariness and reawakened in her chest. "I think we could figure something out." She squeezed his fingers. "Now I'm more certain than ever that God will never leave me. He's promised me that, but I do need to learn to trust Him with whatever is next."

Rhys was so close now their snowshoes touched. He raised her fingers to his warm lips and kissed them. "What might be next on the agenda for you?"

Her face heated. "Well… my next priority is… a soak in that clawfoot tub." She winked and led him down toward the cabin.

"You guys, it looks like a feast." The kitchen island was covered in platters of food, and Carla was ready to eat.

She felt human again after bathing—an indulgence she savored with hot chocolate in hand. Plus she had expressed her gratitude to the two officers who just left the cabin. They'd been kind enough to allow her to come home and freshen up before she gave her official statement alongside Rhys. Back in the forest, she'd been in no state to think clearly when they handed the evidence over. Now, the police knew everything, including details of her initial attack.

While the meeting went on in the living room, Madison and Alexis had stayed in the kitchen preparing food where they were close enough if she needed them but still allowed the officers to do their work.

Now, as Rhys took his turn showering after grabbing a change of clothes from his vehicle, Carla hovered over the charcuterie boards, debating what she was in the mood to eat first.

"We don't have to wait for him, do we?" Alexis popped an olive into her mouth. "I'm starving."

"Rhys won't mind. Let's make a start. I'm famished, too." Carla took a plate and began loading it with a selection of cheeses and meats.

"I'm not surprised, little sister. I still can't believe what an ordeal you've been through." Alexis pushed a steaming mug of milk-laced coffee in front of her. "And Richard Tremblay? I would never have guessed in a million years. It sounds like that poor wife of his was being manipulated by her bully husband and had no real clue why. She did his bidding and slashed Rhys's tires? Bold move in broad daylight."

Madison leaned on the counter. "At least she confessed. I know they've taken her into custody, but I hope she gets some help with her mental health."

"Who knows what else that man was capable of?" Carla shivered and perched on the stool. "Actually, I don't want to think about him again until I have to be in a courtroom."

Madison put an arm around Carla's shoulders. "You can move on now, sweetie. Really move on. Knowing he's where he needs to be and he can't ever hurt you again."

She nodded. "This hasn't been the holiday at home I had imagined. In some ways, it's been everything I could have hoped for." She bit her lower lip and stared at the wedge of brie on her plate. Never in her wildest dreams had she imagined this trip would include kissing Rhys.

"You mean with getting closure?" Alexis sat down next to her at the island. "All the forgiveness and stuff you needed to sort through?"

"For sure. Then there's Rhys…" Her face heated as she thought of him upstairs in her shower.

"What exactly is going on? Do you even know? Is your head even in a space to think rationally today?" Alexis waved a slice of apple in the air. "Madison filled me in about the surprise engagement announcement he sprung on you. What does his fiancée think of him being here with you now?"

Carla took a sip of the latte. "I do need a little space to think it all through, yes, but he's not engaged anymore."

"He's not?" Madison's face lit up.

Carla explained as well as she could what Rhys had told her about his relationship with Gabriella.

"So, he wants to try again with you?" Alexis's eyes narrowed.

She shrugged. "It seems that way."

"It *is* that way."

Carla turned at the sound of Rhys's mellow voice and drank in the sight of him. His hair was still damp, his skin flushed from shower steam, and he'd changed into clean clothes. He looked *good*.

"Ladies, I realize you two are the most important people in Carla's life, and I need you to know my heart."

"O-kay." Alexis's voice oozed skepticism.

"I made the biggest mistake ever when I left Carla. It's taken me two continents, overcoming alcoholism, recommitting my life to God, and even a broken engagement to come to the point where—I want a second chance with her more than anything else. I don't deserve it; I don't deserve her. But I love her." He glanced at Carla. "I've always loved her."

Carla's heart melted, and she glanced at her sister and Madison.

"Oh my." Tears trickled from Madison's eyes.

Alexis raised a brow.

"I don't want to rush you into anything, Carla." He closed the space between them and took both her hands in his. "You need to know how serious I am." He looked over to their kitchen audience and then back at her. "Will you come with me for a minute?"

How serious could this next conversation be? Her cheeks burned. He couldn't be about to propose. He was engaged to another woman yesterday. Alarm bells rang in her head while wedding bells rang in her heart as she slid down from the stool.

God, I've been calling out for a lot of help today, but I need You again...

I will never leave you nor forsake you.

She felt His reassurance in the depths of her soul as she pulled her cardigan tighter across her chest and followed Rhys out through the back door.

"Sit with me?" He patted the wicker love seat laden with fur blankets. "It's the best seat in the house. Or on the back porch."

She looked out at a thousand stars twinkling a welcome to the early winter evening. "I see you orchestrated an exquisite view especially."

He raised a shoulder and winked. "I wanted it to be perfect."

Carla settled into the love seat, and Rhys sat next to her, wrapping a blanket around them both. "Warm enough?"

She nodded and leaned against him, her head on his shoulder, his arm across the back of the love seat.

The porch was lit by myriad white lights, and the outdoor Christmas tree stood guard on their right while the frozen lake stretched out beyond the property on the left. She was safe. They were all safe. She let out a contented sigh.

He stroked her hair in a rhythmical motion until her heavy eyes closed. "Carla, can I ask you something?"

She stiffened. Eyes wide open.

"Don't worry, I'm not expecting you to be my wife tomorrow or anything." He ruffled her hair and let out a chuckle.

She dug her elbow into his ribs. "Well, that's a relief." Although, the way she felt in this moment, she would have said yes, wouldn't she? "In that case, ask away."

"Were you serious when you said your dream would be to settle here in this cabin? That it may be time to move on from your work in Mexico?"

She swivelled to face him. "Yes, but—"

"What if there was a way for you to do that? To work with children—I know it's your passion—and to make this cabin your home. Not just at Christmas, I mean." He ran his free hand down the leg of his jeans, over and over.

Carla frowned. "Rhys Templeton, what are you talking about? You *know* this place is already up for sale. This may be news to you, but I don't exactly make a stack of cash at the orphanage. Plus, there's a definite lack of children up in this area."

He grinned. "I asked you earlier to think about a future with me, and I respect you too much to hurry the process. I also know you need to pray about it. Talk with your friends. Your family. But I was up for hours last night. Thinking and praying. Trying to figure out a solution for your dream to become a reality. I think God may have shown me a way."

What was he talking about? She tilted her head. "And…?"

"And I want to say up front, this solution is not contingent on you and I being a couple."

Her heart sank. Didn't he know how much she longed to be a couple with him?

"I mean, I want a future with you—but with no strings attached. Purely because you love me as much as I love you."

She released the breath she'd been holding and leaned closer to within inches of his nose. "Would you please say what you need to say before I kiss you?"

"I want to buy this place, Carla."

Her jaw dropped. "The cabin?"

"Yes, the cabin. I loved it here, too. I only lived in Hollybrook for a year, but it made a huge impression on me. I've missed it. I've missed that sense of belonging."

"I know what you mean. I've felt the exact same way since I came back. But your business in Seattle?"

"I have a second-in-command who's itching to take over. I have ideas for this place along with some investment capital." He gestured to the empty space at the right side of the property. "I'd like to build a separate, small, private holiday home where kids can stay and play for a stretch of time. Feel loved. Kids affected by alcoholism, like I was. I've run across so many heartbreaking situations in my own journey. I want to give back. Like one man was willing to give back and invest in me. It could be your project." He held both her hands in his. "Or our project."

Carla closed her gaping mouth. "Wow. I wasn't expecting that. Rhys, it sounds amazing."

"Not too crazy?" His eyes flashed, and he gave her hands a quick squeeze. "I've also got dreams of having some kind of culinary school or classes or something when it's not being used by kids. There's lots to figure out, of course, but I want you to know how serious I am about making something work up here. With you, preferably."

In truth, maybe the dream was too crazy.

But maybe not… Maybe this would be the start of a fresh chapter. Just as the cabin had been renovated and renewed, surely, the same could happen with their relationship. Because there was no one she would rather build a future with. No one.

She closed the space between them and kissed him. Hard.

The past five years of agony dispersed like melting snowflakes as she reclaimed this place. This man. Their future.

When they came up for air, her lips tingled with bliss.

"Could I ask *you* a question now?" Carla smirked.

"It's probably going to be yes." He waggled his eyebrows.

"Rhys." She attempted her best bossy voice reserved for the kids at the orphanage.

"Sorry. Of course, ask away." He cupped her cheek in his palm, and she leaned into it.

"I know you have to ride home with Alexis tonight as your car's waiting for new tires. But would you mind staying until after midnight?"

He checked his watch. "Sure. My flight doesn't leave until noon tomorrow. So long as Alexis is up for it, and you're not too exhausted after today."

"Thanks." She settled back down next to him and marveled at the smattering of snowflakes falling against the indigo sky.

"I won't leave until you want me to. May I ask why?"

She rested her head against his shoulder and savored his nearness.

"Because tomorrow is Christmas Eve, and I want to start it with you."

Epilogue

Rhys's stomach was in knots as he stared out across the frozen lake, glistening with a thousand diamonds. Why had Carla asked to meet here today? He tapped the box in his coat pocket, and a shiver ran through him. Partly from the frosty chill in the air but mostly from the anticipation of seeing her again. Was he hoping for too much to think she might give him a second chance?

He hadn't seen Carla since the Seattle party on Boxing Day—and that was a full month ago.

As he'd expected, he barely had time to talk with her while he was busy catering the event, but as he drove her to the airport after, she had gushed about her magical Christmas Day at the cabin and the sister time she enjoyed. Then they shared one last kiss, and she left for Mexico.

He shoved both hands into his pockets and stomped his boots on the snow packed ground. His heart had broken having to say goodbye and let her go, yet he trusted God in this. He had to, didn't he?

Back in the rhythm of his Seattle life, Rhys had buried himself in work to keep from pining like a lovesick teenager while she processed and prayed about her future. He began training his second-in-command to take over, and he researched programs that might be helpful in his project for the cabin property.

He breathed in a deep lungful of fresh mountain air.

His ex was now seeing a mutual friend, and all Rhys could think about was Carla. The cabin. The possibility of a shared dream. And then he'd been surprised by a phone call three days ago from Carla in Mexico with a request to meet him back in Hollybrook.

Now, here he was, at the cabin.

"Rhys?"

He turned from the lake and saw Carla's trim figure jogging toward him through the snow. His smile grew. "Careful. You're not on a Mexican beach, you know."

Her laughter drifted on the frigid winter air.

As she got closer, he could see her beautiful face was now bronzed, and her eyes were bright behind emerald-green framed glasses. She had a joy, a spark he recognized from years ago.

"Come here." He opened his arms, and she fell into them like she belonged there.

He allowed her to take the lead, and she kissed him squarely on the mouth, leaving him breathless.

She pulled back, her arms encircling his waist. "Hi, Rhys. Thanks for coming."

"Are you ever a sight for sore eyes. You look gorgeous."

"Thanks. You don't look so bad yourself."

He arched a brow. "So… are you going to tell me what's going on?"

She took his hand and led him to the back of the cabin. "Sorry about the cloak and dagger stuff."

"It's cool. I love the mysterious. I've missed you." *More than you can imagine.*

Hand-in-hand, they walked up the steps to the back porch and settled onto the wicker sofa. The exact spot where they'd shared a conversation a little over a month ago.

"I've missed you, too. I wanted to speak with you in person about something." Her face grew serious, and his gut clenched.

Carla tried to keep a straight face even though she was ready to burst with joy. She'd missed this man more than she thought possible, and now, as she looked up at his handsome face, her pulse raced.

Like a gift from the past, he pulled her into his arms, and she inhaled his fresh aftershave that reminded her of an ocean breeze. "Is everything all right?" He drew back, and a crease appeared between his brows.

She nodded. *How do I explain all this?* "I did the fleece thing."

He squinted. "The fleece thing?"

"You know how you said you put out a fleece to God and said if we were supposed to give our relationship another chance, that He would make it evidently clear?"

"Oh, that fleece. Yeah, got it." He moved around to fully face her, his hazel eyes wide.

"Well, I wanted to be sure about this cabin. Alexis put it on the market right before Christmas, and so far, no one has taken an interest. It's a slow time of year, so there's that. I was more concerned about moving on from my time in Mexico. God led me there so directly, and He's taught me so much in my years with the kids and through my friendship with Madison and Luke. I was struggling to see how they would get a much-needed replacement in a hurry if I left. I couldn't leave them high and dry. So, my fleece was that God would bring someone along to work there. Because that *never* happens."

"And?" His lips curved into a smile.

She shook her head, and a giggle slipped out. "He did it. He provided the perfect people for the orphanage. Dear friends of Madison and Luke. They're the sweetest couple from Oregon, and they got married a while back on the orphanage beach and ended up adopting one of our babies. It's a long story—but Juliet and Max asked if they could come out for a two-year stint to work as orphanage house parents alongside Madison and Luke. It's perfect." *And an absolute miracle.*

He shook his head and let out a laugh. "Only God…"

"Yes, only God. I've spoken with Luke and Madison, and they're happy with me working until the spring when Juliet, Max, and their little one will arrive in Mexico."

"So, you… you're coming back?" He sat on the edge of the love seat. "You're actually coming back here?"

She nodded and grinned. "There's so much to work out, but yes."

"And this cabin? The project?"

"I happen to know a great realtor, and she gave me a ride up here today." She leaned behind them and knocked on the wall of the cabin.

The back door opened. "Coffee will be ready in a few minutes." Alexis winked and closed the door behind her.

Rhys stood and drew Carla up next to him. "Is this for real?"

She bit her lower lip. "Yes. The only thing is, I can't figure out how this is going to work, with you buying the cabin, your dream of making it something where we can make a difference in the lives of kids, all these plans—unless we're a couple. You know what I mean?" She batted her lashes.

His eyes bugged. "Is there another fleece story?"

She reached up and put her hands around his neck. "I don't think I need any more confirmation, Rhys. I know it in my heart." She ran her fingertips through his thick hair. "You're my person—and this is my place."

He smothered her in a hug and then pulled back to look deep into her eyes. "I'm going to do this properly. Give it all to God first. Let you have all the time you need. I'll plan a proposal fit for my princess. The perfect ring. Then we can plan the wedding of your dreams." He pulled her into a kiss that took her breath away. "I can't wait—but I *will* wait."

She blew out a stream of air and straightened her glasses. "I agree. There's no hurry. This is all fresh and new."

"Even though it's familiar and comforting?"

"All of that."

He reached into the inside pocket of his wool coat. "I have something special for you. A late Christmas present, but you can also think of it as a promise for our future together."

Her fingers itched to see what was inside the tiny velvet box. She opened it and gasped.

A silver snowflake pendant on a delicate chain sparkled in the winter sunshine.

"It's perfect, Rhys, thank you so much." She kissed his cheeks, and then his lips again. Fresh, new, familiar, and comforting. "I'm going to wear this every single day until we're together again."

"A snowflake in Mexico. I like it. It'll keep you sparkling until I can put a ring on your finger."

Lord, thank You. This feels so right.

God's grace had led Carla back to this very place. To this man. To this moment.

Tears pooled in her eyes, and snowflakes began to fall as Carla and Rhys turned and made their way into the cabin.

Their cabin.

If you enjoyed this book, please consider leaving a review on your favorite retailer. It's such a blessing and help to me!

About the Author

A published, award-winning Christian author, Laura writes heartwarming encouragement for your soul— especially in her numerous romantic suspense novels, as well as her teen fiction, marriage, and children's books. Laura is a hope*writers certified writing coach, a book-loving chocoholic mom and nanny, and is married to her high school sweetheart. Originally from the UK, they now live the empty nest life in Kelowna, British Columbia, with their French bulldog!

www.laurathomasauthor.com

www.ingramcontent.com/pod-product-compliance
Lightning Source LLC
Chambersburg PA
CBHW071933190726
48293CB00004B/1253